MIRROR MAGIC

Books by Claire Fayers

The Accidental Pirates:
Voyage to Magical North
Journey to Dragon Island

MIRROR MAGIC

CLAIRE FAYERS

ILLUSTRATED BY BECKA MOOR

MACMILLAN CHILDREN'S BOOKS

For Linda, who loves books

First published 2018 by Macmillan Children's Books
an imprint of Pan Macmillan
20 New Wharf Road, London N1 9RR
Associated companies throughout the world
www.panmacmillan.com

ISBN 978-1-5098-7006-6

135798642

A CIP catalogue record for this book is available from
the British Library.

Printed and bound by CPI Group (UK) Ltd, Croydon CR0 4YY

These are the terms of the covenant between the Human World and the Unworld.

The Fair Folk will withdraw from the world and take all magic with them to form their own realm. Yet the Human World must not be left wholly without magic. Magic mirrors will be created, two by two, each pair forming a doorway between the Human World and the new Unworld. Any person may cross through, if invited from the other side. Furthermore, the Unworld will supply all magical goods and services requested through the mirrors.

While the mirrors stand, so shall this covenant. If it ends, the Unworld will end with it. What is written must come to pass.

Mr Matthew Harcourt
7 Mill Lane
Cambridge

16 June 1852

Dear Mr Harcourt,
My deep and sincere condolences on your loss.
I knew your parents well and I learned of their
passing with great sadness.

It has come to my attention that you are facing
some financial hardship. I am in need of a clerk
at my offices here in Wyse and it would please
me greatly if you would consider accepting the
position.

I recall that you have a sister, who will be eleven
or twelve years of age now, and my invitation
extends to her, also. I will have no trouble securing
her a suitable position in a household in Wyse.

I look forward to welcoming you at your
earliest convenience.
Yours sincerely,

Lord Ephraim Skinner

Her Majesty's Government, Taxation and
Compliance (Unworld)
Waning Crescent, Wyse, England

CHAPTER 1

The town of Wyse, set precisely on the border of England and Wales, is remarkable for one thing: it is the only remaining human town where magic works. Or it will be, in the mid-nineteenth century. As for other time periods, don't ask me: I'm only a book.

The Book

Ava leaned out of the carriage window as the road wound and ducked between the rolling hills to Wyse. The English countryside appeared disappointingly ordinary.

'I don't see any enchantments,' she said.

Matthew gave her a tired smile. 'You will soon enough. Just wait a while.'

But she didn't want to wait, not when everything else in the world seemed to rush on so fast. Ava sat back down, wriggling her feet in between a pair of boxes. Six months – it sounded like a long time but it felt like nothing. In six months, their lives had fallen apart, their parents taken by typhoid fever, their home sold to pay their debts. And now, travelling in a borrowed coach, with their last belongings stacked around them, they were headed back to the town they'd left behind when she was two years old.

'You still haven't told me what Lord Skinner is like,' she said, trying to distract herself from her thoughts. She didn't remember him at all, but lately every time she thought about him she had the uncomfortable feeling that she was suffocating.

Matthew rubbed a hand over his eyes. 'I don't remember much about him either. He was large, and wore fancy clothes. Everyone liked him.'

'Father didn't.' A tight pain knitted together in Ava's chest. *Stay away from mirrors, Ava.* Father's words as he lay, feverish. And then, muttered over and over: *Don't trust Lord Skinner. He's not what he seems.*

'Father was sick,' Matthew said. 'He didn't know what he was saying.'

'But it is still strange. Father saying his name out of the blue like that so soon before he . . .' Ava took a breath. 'Before he died. And then the letter coming. It's almost as if Lord Skinner was watching us.'

'That's just silly. No doubt he heard the news from a relative in Wyse. It's hardly a secret.' Matthew's voice had an edge to it now. 'We have work and a home, even if it's not what you would like. Let's be thankful.'

'I know. I'm sorry.' She hadn't meant to upset

Matthew. Her hand crept up to the mark on her left cheek – a thin moon-shaped crescent, left over from a measles rash, or so her parents had said. Even back home in Cambridgeshire, however, almost as far from Wyse and magic as you could get, Ava had caught people looking at her oddly and whispering about fairy marks.

Because, of course, Father had been a conjuror once. He had owned one of the few working magic mirrors left in the world. Father, who never gave orders or raised his voice, had summoned fairies from the Unworld to do his bidding.

Ava's imagination failed when she thought about it. Her father had never talked about life in Wyse, only saying he'd sold the magic mirror to his nephew, along with everything else, and it was best forgotten. Yet something must have happened to make him abandon that life. Why would you choose to live somewhere ordinary like Cambridgeshire when you could be living in the last magical town in all of Britain?

The carriage bounced and jiggled over holes in the road, taking them ever closer to Wyse. Ava kicked her heels against her seat. 'If Father hadn't moved away from Wyse, you might be a conjuror now.'

Matthew groaned and shook his head. 'For the last time, I'm quite happy to be a clerk.' He frowned at her. 'And you'll be happy with whatever Lord Skinner finds for you. We can't afford to be choosy.'

Ava shrugged, looking back out of the window. Matthew might think himself lucky to be a clerk, but a position in a household for her? Ava wanted more than that. They were coming home to Wyse – town of magic mirrors. If she could find Father's mirror, if she could stand in front of it just for a moment, who knew what she might see?

But then she forgot everything because, as the carriage reached the top of the hill, she caught her first glimpse of Wyse.

From the pictures Ava had seen, she'd expected the town to glitter as if it was made of gold and fine jewels. Instead, it looked more as if a child had put it together out of cheap glass. A dizzying array of colours bled across the buildings, smearing from red to green to yellow. The narrow roads that wound between were pale silver and gave off a sticky gleam like slug trails.

If this was what fairy magic looked like, Ava didn't think much of it.

'I thought you said Wyse was the grandest town in Britain,' she said.

Matthew leaned out of his window to see. An open-top carriage came towards them, heading out of the town. It shimmered with a rainbow of bright jewels and the four ladies inside boasted golden skin and hair in various shades of green. A faint haze surrounded them all as if Ava was seeing them through a light mist. She rubbed her eyes, but the mist remained. The ladies waved and giggled, their hands leaving gold streaks in the air.

Matthew raised his hat and waved back, making the ladies giggle even harder.

'It doesn't even look real,' Ava complained.

'It's not supposed to – that's the whole point.' Matthew replaced his hat. 'Fairy enchantments always have a coloured aura, especially the cheaper ones. It's just a bit of fun.'

People thought it was fun to drive around in carriages looking blurry? Ava picked at the edge of her seat as their own carriage rattled on past a patch of overgrown parkland and over a narrow stone bridge into the centre of town. Some of the buildings they passed were large and grand, four or five storeys tall, with high, arched windows, but they all looked as if they needed a good clean beneath the shimmering layer of enchantments. Some were quite obviously empty, with birds nesting on the chimneys and trails of ivy crossing the fronts. Even the theatre, which was supposed to be the sixth largest in the country, seemed dejected, covered in peeling posters.

Mr Radcot, gentleman conjuror. All wishes guaranteed.

(*All* wishes, Ava wondered, or just wishes for fake-looking enchantments?)

Mr Edmund Footer, conjuror by royal appointment to Queen Victoria. Private audiences granted Monday–Friday.

Langhile and Gaddesby, conjurors. Children's parties a speciality (ask about our summer offers).

Ava tried to imagine Father's name on a poster. *Alfred Harcourt, conjuror. Special offers on Fridays and Saturdays.*

'Mr Edmund Footer is our cousin,' Matthew said, touching Ava's arm. 'He's the one who bought Father's mirror before we left Wyse. I always felt sorry for him; his mother is horrible.'

His mother – their aunt. More people Ava had never met. They hadn't even come to the funeral, though Aunt Lily had sent condolences.

Then Ava spotted a group of people standing outside the theatre holding signs that read *Fair Folk: People, not Fairies* and *Ban All Conjurors.*

'Who are they?' she asked, forgetting about the Footers.

A boy left the group and ran after the carriage. 'Freedom for Fair Folk,' he said, shoving a leaflet into Ava's hand. 'We meet every Thursday. Number two, Church Street, behind the town hall. Fair Folk are people too.'

He ran back to join the small group of protesters. Ava watched him go. He looked about her own age, and his smile had been friendly, but what would he say if he knew she was a conjuror's daughter? She bet he wouldn't be half so friendly then. She tucked the leaflet into the top of one of their luggage bags. Why would people protest on behalf of fairies, anyway? '*Are* fairies real people?' she asked.

Matthew gave an indifferent shrug. 'Father always said they were, and he should know, I guess. Whatever they are, though, they're not like us. I wouldn't trust them.'

'I'm not suggesting we trust them. I just want to see one.' She flashed him a smile. 'Where's your sense of adventure?'

Matthew used to say that to her all the time – *Where's your sense of adventure, Ava?* Usually it was just before he dared her to do something she shouldn't, like climbing a tree or stealing the treacle tart Mother was saving for supper. She was too cautious, Matthew had always said. She needed to learn to take risks. When had that changed? Had it been when their parents fell ill, or maybe at the funeral when Matthew suddenly seemed to understand he was head of the family? Or when he'd realized exactly how much money they owed?

Or was it her fault? Matthew could have got by far more easily on his own. As a young, single gentleman, even without money, he could have taken a job anywhere he pleased. A young sister in tow made everything twice as difficult. As he said, he couldn't afford to be choosy any more.

Ava leaned out of the carriage. 'Excuse me,' she called to the driver. 'Can we stop here a moment?'

The driver glanced back at them and scowled, but he pulled on the reins, stopping the horses.

'What are you doing?' Matthew asked.

'I want to have a look around. Are you coming?'

She slipped out of the carriage before Matthew could stop her.

The protesters were still chanting behind her. Ava was careful not to look in case they thought she was interested in joining them. She crossed the road to a shop with a gold sign that flashed on and off.

Wyse Emporium of Souvenirs, Mirrors and Magical Goods.

Underneath the main sign, a smaller one, written on paper said: *Breakages must be paid for. Fairy magic is illusion only. It does not change reality. It is not permanent and will fade with use. No refunds.*

The shelves in the window were crowded with miniature silver mirrors, china tea sets and cheap-looking jewellery, all hazy with fairy enchantments.

'Are these the kind of enchantments Father used to order?' Ava asked as Matthew joined her.

'He supplied some of the shops,' Matthew said. 'The shopkeepers used to bring their lists to the house and Father would go into his room and order everything through the mirror.' He sighed, remembering. 'And then the goods would appear in his room, all neatly packed.'

'And then he decided to stop. Just like that?'

'So he said.' Matthew tilted his hat back and rubbed a hand over his face. He looked far too pale in his mourning clothes. He'd spent so much time looking after her that he'd forgotten to look after himself, Ava reflected, and again the unwanted thought crept in: He'd be better off without her.

She slipped her hand through his arm. 'Never mind. Shall we go inside?'

A bell jingled as Matthew opened the shop door. Ava edged round a shelf, holding her skirt out of the way. A few tourists were browsing through the goods on display and the shopkeeper watched from behind a silver counter. *More like cheap wood enchanted to look like silver*, Ava thought, noticing patches of plain brown beneath the haze. She felt the shopkeeper's gaze skim over her, resting slightly too long on the mark on her cheek.

'I have a beautifying enchantment that will get rid of that for you,' he said.

Ava stared straight at him. 'Get rid of what?' She smiled when he flushed and looked away.

Matthew picked up a mirror. '*A present from Wyse*,' he said, reading the inscription on the back. 'I thought they came from the Unworld.'

The shopkeeper's moustache bristled. 'Our mirrors

are very popular. A reminder of your holiday perhaps?'

'We're not on holiday.' Matthew put the mirror back and raised his hat. 'Matthew Harcourt. My family used to live here.'

The shopkeeper stood up straight. 'You're Harcourt's son? So you're going to be working for Lord Skinner. He's a fine gentleman. My youngest son has been trying to get a job at Waning Crescent for years.'

He made it sound like an accusation, as if Matthew had deliberately stolen his son's job.

'And she must be the girl,' the shopkeeper added, staring at Ava.

Ava tugged at her skirt, the black crepe suddenly feeling tight and too hot. She picked up another mirror. This one had a poem on the bottom.

When you're angry, when you're sad,
Put it in the mirror and you won't feel so bad.

'What's that supposed to mean?' she asked.

'It's a nursery rhyme,' the shopkeeper said. 'It doesn't mean anything.'

'It finishes, *Let the mirror take your pain and you will be quite happy again*,' Matthew added. 'I remember it from when I was a child.'

Ava wished she could put all her bad feeling into a mirror. She stared into the cheap glass, tilting it this way and that.

'You don't want to look too long into mirrors around here,' the shopkeeper said. 'You never know what you might see.' He smirked as Ava jumped and set the mirror down. 'Just kidding. There's a fairy enchantment on it to make it glow a bit but underneath it's common glass. Two shillings, if you want to buy it.'

He held his hand out for the money. Ava shook her head and turned away. She felt the shopkeeper still staring at her until one of the other customers asked to buy a milk jug. Ava shut her eyes and let out a breath. She wished she hadn't come in now.

Matthew dug in his pocket for a calling card and set it on the counter. 'We'll be living at number eight, Primrose Hill. We're looking forward to making the acquaintance of our neighbours.'

'I'm sure you are,' the shopkeeper said, ignoring Matthew's card. 'Well, no doubt you have many things to do today. Good day to you both.'

'He was horrible,' Ava said as they climbed back into the carriage. She didn't feel like going into any of the other shops. The horses started off with a jolt that threw her back into her seat. 'Did you see how he looked at me?'

Matthew threw a glance behind. 'He's cross because I got a job with Lord Skinner and his son didn't. Don't let one rude man spoil things for you.'

For a moment he sounded more like his old self and Ava allowed herself a cautious smile. Maybe coming back to Wyse would be good for them after all.

The carriage moved on, past the row of shops, and up a hill, where the driver stopped about halfway up.

'This is it,' he said. 'Number eight.'

The house didn't look too bad. The garden was overgrown, but there were apple trees and probably a vegetable patch under the weeds. Dark tendrils of ivy swarmed up the front of the house and on to the roof where they appeared to be attempting to strangle the chimney.

The coachman grunted and jumped down. 'You'll have to carry your bags in from here.'

He didn't offer to help and Ava didn't ask. No point causing extra work for him when they could manage on their own. She grabbed two of the smaller bags and hauled them along the path.

Inside the house, the hallway smelled of damp. Patches of grey mould stained one wall, and an old rug lay in a dirty heap to one side. Each room was the same: grimy, damp and musty. On the other hand, they were large, and the whole house was theirs. Ava felt a stirring of excitement.

'It's not too bad,' Ava said, running her finger across the dirt on a window. Everything would need cleaning, but they could drag the carpets outside and beat them, and if they opened all the windows, the smell would soon go.

The kitchen had an old stove that looked like it might work, and a table and four chairs. And, propped up on the table, against a covered milk jug, was a letter.

Dear Mr and Miss Harcourt,
Welcome to your new home. I hope you will
be comfortable here. I am sorry I was not able
to greet you on arrival. However, I would like
to invite you both to dine with me at Waning
Crescent this evening. I shall expect you at seven
o'clock.
 Yours sincerely,
 Lord Skinner

The paper was plain, heavyweight, unenchanted, and the letter itself was written in a strong hand with no excess flourishes. It was handwriting you could trust.

Don't trust Lord Skinner, her father had said. Reading the letter again, Ava felt suffocated.

'We should have bought food while we were in town,' Matthew said, coming into the kitchen. 'Tomorrow's Sunday and everything will be shut. Do you want to run back and get some supplies while I start unpacking?' He noticed the piece of paper in Ava's hand. 'What's that?'

She handed it to him, her hand trembling a little. 'An invitation, I think – or a summons.'

CHAPTER 2

When you're angry, when you're sad,
Put it in the mirror and you won't feel so bad.
Let your reflection take your pain
And you will be quite happy again.
You shouldn't say things like that to children.
Children will believe anything.

(Yes, I know the last two lines don't rhyme. I'm not a poetry
book, all right?)

The Book

Wyse's high street was quieter when Ava walked
back along it, looking for the bakery. The
protesters in front of the theatre had dispersed, leaving
a scattering of crumpled leaflets on the ground. Ava
kicked one aside, her bag bumping heavily over her
shoulder as she walked. She kept her head down,
pretending not to notice when people turned to watch
her walk past.

'That's her,' she heard one man say. 'The one
who . . . You know.'

But when Ava turned to ask what he meant, the whole group was hurrying away.

'Excuse me,' Ava called after them loudly. They turned back, looking at each other and the pavement, anywhere except at Ava. She smiled sweetly at them. 'Could you tell me the way to the baker's, please?'

The relief that flooded their faces as they pointed down a side road was so intense that Ava had to bite her lip to stop herself giggling.

Turning on to the road, she spotted the baker's shop halfway along. It looked empty, but the door opened when she pushed it.

'Hello, are you open? My brother and I have just moved here, and . . .'

A head popped up from behind the counter. Ava blinked. 'And we need bread,' she finished. 'I saw you before. You gave me a leaflet.'

The boy grinned, his round face dimpling. 'Yes, I did.' He wiped his hands on his shirt and held one out over the counter to shake. 'Charles Brunel. Of Brunel and Son's Bakery – that's my father and me. My mother runs Freedom for Fair Folk.'

He stared hard at her as they shook hands, his gaze taking in the smudges on her dress, then flicking up to her face. Ava saw him notice her measles mark, but he didn't react to it with the usual curiosity or embarrassment; he just gave it a quick look and went on to study the rest of her.

'It's actually quite rude to stare,' Ava said, drawing her hand back.

'Sorry. I don't get much chance to practise.'

'You practise staring?' She shook her head. She could feel herself getting drawn into a conversation she didn't want right now. 'Never mind,' she said. 'Can I just have some bread?'

Charles turned and started pushing bread rolls into a paper bag. 'Everyone's talking about you,' he said. 'Matthew and Ava Harcourt. They're wondering what you're doing back here. They think your brother must have bribed Lord Skinner into offering you work – either that or you cast an enchantment on him.' He spun the bag to seal it, watching Ava out of the corner of his eye.

She raised her chin and glared at him. 'My parents died of typhoid fever,' she said stiffly, 'then Matthew and I ran out of money and we had to move. Lord Skinner offered Matthew a job so we came here. If we could have afforded a bribe we wouldn't have needed to come. As for casting an enchantment, do I *look* like a conjuror?'

Charles set the bag down and rested his arms on the counter. 'No, but you should never judge by appearances. That's the first thing you learn if you're a policeman.'

'A policeman?' Ava looked about at the flour-dusted shelves. 'I thought this was a bakery.'

'It is. I'm helping out here for now, but I'm going to be a policeman when I grow up. We just got our first constable in Wyse and it's amazing. You get to wear a uniform and help solve crimes. Is it true you nearly died of measles once?'

Ava put a hand involuntarily to her cheek. 'I *had* measles when I was two. I don't know about nearly dying. I should go. We're having dinner with Lord Skinner this evening.'

'Really?' Charles's smile faltered and quickly recovered. 'I'm sure you'll like him. Everyone does.'

'You don't sound like you do,' Ava said.

Charles shrugged. 'I don't really know him. But being a policeman is all about noticing the details.' He handed her the bag of bread rolls. 'Everyone says Lord Skinner is a fine gentleman – but they say exactly that, like they've learned the words or something. And there's this funny smell sometimes.'

'A smell?'

'You'll see what I mean. Watch for the things other people might miss. The truth is in the detail. There's no charge for the bread. Welcome to Wyse.'

Charles's words echoed in Ava's mind as she paused at the entrance to Waning Crescent later that evening. A pair of iron gates stood open, leading to a wide, curved avenue with a semicircle of lawn surrounded by tall, white houses. None of the street lamps were lit yet, except a pair halfway along, which burned with a flickering, pale green light.

'Fairy lights,' Matthew said. 'I remember them.' He looked less sure of himself now that he was standing outside his new employer's house.

Ava shivered as a breeze tugged at her best dress. She wrapped her shawl closer.

'I could tell Lord Skinner you're ill if you don't want to come,' Matthew said.

Ava shook her head. She couldn't let Matthew face Lord Skinner on his own. Besides, after what Charles had said, she was curious to see him.

They walked along the crescent until they came to the fairy lights, which stood either side of a vast pair of doors.

'Here goes,' Matthew said, and tugged the bell pull.

The doors opened so quickly that Lord Skinner must have been waiting behind them. Ava stepped back in surprise.

Matthew had said Lord Skinner was large, but the man who opened the door wasn't just large – he was enormous. His jacket flapped around him, big enough to fit twenty people inside it, and his blue velvet waistcoat strained over his vast stomach. Rolls of fat drooped from his chin and wobbled when he moved his head. Even his feet were fat, overflowing out of shiny, black shoes.

'Mr Harcourt,' he said, holding out a hand

to Matthew. 'Welcome. I am Lord Skinner. My condolences for your loss.'

Surely lords didn't open their own doors? Ava realized she'd been staring and curtsied quickly, her face burning.

Lord Skinner offered her his hand too. His hands were surprisingly thin compared to the rest of him, his slender fingers as dry as old paper, and he gripped Ava so hard that it hurt. So far everything about him felt solid and reassuringly real, not a single hint of fairy enchantments. She guessed he was about forty or fifty but it was hard to tell. His hair was greying, but only around his ears. He smelled quite normal too – Charles must have been making that up to tease her.

'Come along in,' Lord Skinner said, releasing her. 'Time and supper wait for no man.'

Ava glanced at Matthew. He seemed different, happier. Some of the worry lines had faded from his face, making him look younger. He already liked Lord Skinner, Ava thought, and why shouldn't he when Lord Skinner seemed perfectly fine? Father and Charles had both been wrong, and she was glad – glad to see Matthew smiling again.

Eagerly she followed Matthew through the doors into Waning Crescent.

There, she stopped dead.

The hall was full of mirrors. A jumble of different-sized silver frames hung from floor to ceiling.

Chandeliers swayed overhead and the reflected candlelight blazed so that Ava almost felt as if she was stepping into a fire – except for the cold. Even the warmth of all the candles couldn't mask the chill. She turned slowly, seeing her face everywhere, the pale mark on her cheek standing out.

'Waning Crescent used to be a museum of fairy magic,' Lord Skinner said, smiling at her confusion. 'These are all old magic mirrors, their magic long dead. When I moved back to Wyse, I decided to keep them all as reminders of the past.'

Look for the details, Charles had said. Looking about, Ava noticed marks on the wall where several mirrors looked as if they had been rearranged. She ran her fingers across one of them, wondering what magic glass felt like. It felt just like ordinary glass, but then the mirror no longer worked. Perhaps an active one would feel different.

'You won't be seeing any fairies in them, I'm afraid,' Lord Skinner said, smiling. He paused to the side of the mirror. 'Are you interested in fairy magic, Miss Harcourt?'

Ava jerked her hand away from the glass, embarrassed he'd caught her looking.

'My sister is at the age where she's interested in everything,' Matthew said drily. 'My apologies.'

'Not at all. Curiosity should be encouraged in the young.'

Ava shot a triumphant smile at Matthew. Lord Skinner didn't seem so bad, after all.

'Do you know why the mirrors stopped working, Lord Skinner?' she asked.

Lord Skinner walked on down the hall. 'No one does. There are various theories – the Industrial Revolution meant we no longer needed magic and so it dwindled through lack of use. Or maybe the mirrors were never meant to last forever. We have six working mirrors in Wyse now – that's all. Six conjurors who supply all the souvenir shops and ensure the town appears suitably magical for the holidaymakers. I oversee the legal and taxation side of things and make sure the conjurors follow proper health and safety requirements.'

He didn't look at any of the mirrors as he walked past them, Ava noticed, but led them on annoyingly quickly when she wanted to linger and look at them all. Only six working mirrors left, out of hundreds.

'What will happen if the last mirrors stop working?' Ava asked.

Lord Skinner spread his hands in a helpless shrug. 'Then Wyse will be just an ordinary town, and I . . .' His gaze drifted. 'Well, the mirrors have lasted so far. Let's hope they continue to do so. Now, I'm sure you're both hungry. This way.'

A pair of servants opened the doors at the end of the hallway and stood aside to let them through. Ava stole a glance at one of them, an old man. He stood stiffly to attention, not even looking at her as she walked past.

'This is the banqueting hall,' Lord Skinner said. 'I normally reserve it for government functions, but I thought we'd eat here tonight.'

Ava shivered as she looked around. The room was vast and, although the fireplace was almost as tall as she was, the warmth from the fire barely reached her. Arched windows overlooked the lawns outside and a table stretched the length of the room, but there were only three places set, at the end closest to the fire.

'Please do sit down,' Lord Skinner said, squeezing himself into the chair at the head of the table. Most of himself, anyway.

More servants appeared through a door at the corner of the room, so quietly they might have come out of thin air. Ava watched as one poured water into glasses and another placed a soup plate in front of her.

He's not what he seems, Father had said. It didn't matter to Ava whether Charles was wrong or not, but could Father have been wrong as well?

Lord Skinner took a big gulp from his spoon, swallowing noisily. 'You'll find Wyse a friendly town once people get to know you,' he said. 'By the way, Miss Harcourt, you will be pleased to know that I have secured you a position as housemaid with Mr Edmund Footer, your cousin, and his mother.'

Ava dropped her spoon with a clatter. She bent to

retrieve it and found one of the servants was already there.

'Sorry. Mr Footer and his mother? Didn't they buy Father's house?'

Lord Skinner nodded, apparently oblivious to the storm of anxiety inside her. 'The house, the furnishings and your father's magic mirror, of course. I did wonder whether you might mind going to your old home as a maid, but then I reasoned you probably wouldn't remember it. You were so young when you left.' He broke a bread roll in two and reached for the butter dish. 'Better to work within the family if possible, I thought.'

Something sharpened in his eyes – something cold and hungry. At the same moment, a waft of strange scent surrounded her – damp ground and old leaves and something Ava couldn't identify, though she was sure she'd smelled it many times before. Her chest tightened.

Then a servant slipped a clean soup spoon beside Ava's hand and as she moved to pick it up the scent faded. She'd probably imagined it, she thought. What did it matter where she went to work? As Lord Skinner said, better to be with family than strangers.

'That sounds perfect,' she said. 'Thank you.'

Lord Skinner sat back. 'Excellent. You are to start work there on Monday morning. Tomorrow, you may wish to attend church, but if you prefer to stay home and settle yourselves in I'm sure no one will think any the less of you. Now, tell me about yourself, Mr Harcourt. Your parents settled in Cambridgeshire – that's a long way from Wyse.'

The conversation continued. The soup bowls were quietly collected and fish appeared, then a whole side of roast beef. Lord Skinner carved it himself into thick slices that oozed red juices. The servants cleared their plates and set down trays of blancmange and sponge cake.

Ava sat quietly. She didn't know why Charles had warned her about Lord Skinner. He was a fine gentleman. She caught herself. *A fine gentleman. They say it like they've learned the words or something.*

She realized Lord Skinner had spoken to her and she jerked her head up. 'I'm sorry, I . . .'

'I was telling Mr Harcourt about the theatre,' Lord Skinner said. He put a forkful of chocolate sponge cake into his mouth. 'You should go to see a conjuring show when you have the opportunity. I'm sure you'd find it interesting.'

His faded blue eyes sharpened again. Had he guessed she dreamed of conjuring? Ava shifted in her seat. 'Mirrors are handed down through families, aren't they? Is that why Mr Footer is able to use Father's – because he's his nephew?'

Matthew coughed pointedly, but Lord Skinner didn't seem to mind the question. If anything, he looked pleased at Ava's interest. 'That's right. Mirrors are usually passed down from father to son, but they don't have to be. It is said that the original conjurors had some fairy blood in them, which was why they could use the mirrors, and that ability runs through families.'

Through families? Then that meant . . .

Lord Skinner nodded as if guessing her thoughts. 'Your father was a conjuror, Miss Harcourt, and that means you have fairy blood in you. What do you think about that?'

Matthew laughed. 'By your reasoning, I have fairy blood too, and anyone who's descended from a conjuror. That's probably half of Wyse, at least. You may even have fairy blood yourself, Lord Skinner. We could all use magic mirrors if we wanted to.'

Ava scowled. Trust Matthew to make the whole thing sound ordinary. That odd smell came back, just for a moment, and she stifled a yawn, suddenly exhausted, as if all the rich food she'd eaten was weighing her down.

'Do forgive me,' Lord Skinner said. 'As I said, my interest is merely administrative. I'm happy to leave magic to the conjurors.' He stood up. 'Well, it's late and you've had a long journey today. I'll have my carriage take you home.'

Ava's head swam as she climbed into the waiting carriage and it wasn't just because of the rich meal.

She couldn't decide what she thought about Lord Skinner at all. He seemed nice, perfectly normal, not somebody to beware of. And yet . . .

'He's a fine gentleman,' Matthew murmured.

Ava stiffened. 'What did you say?'

'Lord Skinner. He's a fine gentleman, don't you think?'

Ava did think it. The words lodged in her head as if she'd memorized them, just like Charles had said. She folded her arms, trying to think of something else. 'I don't believe he's not interested in magic. Waning Crescent is practically a museum of magic with all those mirrors. He's supposed to be the minister in charge of magic. If you're in charge of something, you should be interested in it.'

'Not if you're in the government,' Matthew said drily.

'Be serious. Father said not to trust him. Are you saying we should ignore Father?'

'No, I'm saying . . . I don't know. Lord Skinner seemed perfectly reasonable to me. Let's give him a chance, all right?'

Ava nodded reluctantly. They were stuck here for now, and they had to make the best of things.

Beyond the iron gates, all the street lights were burning now with a green-golden glow that made the whole crescent appear like something out of another world.

CHAPTER 3

I bet you're wondering when we'll get on to the fairies. Don't deny it – I know what you're thinking: I am a mind-reading, future-seeing book from across the mirror, after all. Human creatures are all the same – only interested in the magic. Come on, then. You might as well take a look at what's happening in Unwyse while there's still time. In case everyone dies.

The Book

Howell hated going out on Sundays. It was the one day of the week humans didn't send orders through the mirrors, and the streets of Unwyse were full of people doing their own shopping. Already, he'd been shoved, stood on and elbowed aside more times than he could count.

He'd hoped the square outside the Mirror Station would be quieter, but a queue snaked back and forth: people waiting to hand over goods for delivery through the mirrors first thing Monday morning. Smoke from the nearby chimneys of Waxing Gibbous mingled with the silver mist, occasionally forming shapes of flowers and leaves where magic pooled in the still air. The mist was always heaviest around the Station, and today it had the stink of gone-off eggs.

Tucking his bag under his arm, Howell began to edge his way through.

'Watch it,' a man snapped. 'I've got a hundred enchanted roses here. Special order for tomorrow.'

'Sorry,' Howell said, not sorry at all. The man had all day to deliver his boxes to the Station so why do it now?

A boy in a red uniform was checking people's papers at the Station doors and Howell paused to watch. *I could do that job*, he thought with a stab of jealousy; you didn't need any special skill with magic to keep order here. No chance of that, though, when the station guards were all hand-picked by Mr Bones.

Mr Bones, who owned the Mirror Station, and most of Unwyse with it. Everyone, on their eleventh birthday, began a year's apprenticeship in Mr Bones's factory, Waxing Gibbous, where most of the enchantments for the human world were created. It was a chance to be useful, but, more than that, a chance for people to explore their talents and find out what they were good at.

Howell, it had turned out, wasn't particularly good at anything. While other people pulled magic from the air to turn dead leaves into roses, or learned how to change their own appearance, Howell remained stubbornly Howell-like.

During his apprenticeship, he'd ended up doing all the jobs that no one wanted. Eight-hour shifts of sweeping floors and cleaning machinery in suffocating, numbing boredom. He'd hoped someone might notice how hard he worked and give him a chance at a better job, but nobody did.

When his year had finally ended three months ago, his parents found him a job where his lack of magical talent wouldn't matter and, satisfied that he could take care of himself, they'd left Unwyse to go travelling. Howell hadn't seen them since. He missed them sometimes, but mostly he was just annoyed that they'd left him behind.

He tore his gaze away from the factory chimneys. Best not to think about Waxing Gibbous. He was out now and it was unlikely he'd go back.

A lady in a startlingly large hat full of blue roses bumped into him. 'Oh, sorry,' she said, then she pushed back the brim of her hat and stared at him. 'Excuse me, aren't you . . .'

'In a hurry,' Howell said. He'd suddenly had enough of this crowd. The lady was still trying to talk to him, but he hurried away from her, pushing his way on through groups of people and ignoring their shouts as he trod on bags and boxes.

Slipping around the statue of Mr Bones at the edge

of the square, Howell stopped to catch his breath and then walked on. He avoided Euphorbia Lane where mad Madame Brille lived – last time he went that way the old lady had threatened to turn him into an earwig – and cut through the clothes market instead. He came out the other side on to an almost empty road.

The mist was thinner here and smelled of grass with a hint of smoke, as if someone had been making summer bonfires. The few people strolling by seemed in less of a hurry. Howell took a pastry out of his bag and ate as he walked, licking the crumbs off his fingers.

Halfway along the road, between an office and a shop selling cheese, he came to a building with a front made entirely of glass.

Here it was: the one place in Unwyse where his lack of magical talent wasn't a problem. Howell finished his pastry, glanced up at the sign over the door and sighed.

Welcome to the House of Forgotten Mirrors.

The mirror gallery was deserted, holding only a vast collection of old mirrors, gathered from all over the Unworld, none of them working. Wrapped in white sheets, they looked like a congregation of ghosts.

Howell put the bag on the counter and shrugged his coat off.

Before he could even hang it up, another boy came thumping down the stairs. His hair was a paler shade of green than Howell's and lay greased flat to show off the tips of his ears.

Howell groaned silently. Trust Will to be awake now, just in time to steal all the breakfast.

'You're late,' Will said, snatching the bag and rummaging inside. 'What were you doing?'

'There was a queue at the baker's. Where's Master Tudur?'

Will pulled a muffin out of the bag and stuffed half of it into his mouth. 'Gone to visit his mother. You can clean the mirrors today. I've got work to do upstairs.'

You've got sleeping to do upstairs, more like, Howell thought. Will outranked him, being two years older and with an irritating and quite useless magical talent for mimicking birdsong. But in Unwyse even useless was better than non-existent.

Howell shrugged and hung his coat on the stand by the desk. 'I cleaned all the mirrors last week and nothing's happened to them since. I thought Master Tudur said I had to tidy upstairs today.'

'I'm doing that instead.' Will tucked the bag of pastries under his arm. 'I'll leave you one of these for later.'

No he wouldn't. Will would eat the lot, then fall asleep again, and when Master Tudur came back he'd blame Howell for not getting the work done.

Will pushed him aside and went back up the stairs. Howell heard his feet thump overhead, and then the creak of the bed. He slumped into Master Tudur's chair behind the counter. He might as well copy Will and have a rest. It wasn't as if the mirrors needed cleaning again.

For a while, Howell watched people passing in the street outside, but nobody stopped or even looked at the house. Master Tudur liked to pretend that this place was something like the museums in the human world – a reminder of Unworld history. Really, though, it was just a storehouse for things that were no longer needed or wanted. Howell let his gaze drift down the rows of mirrors, hundreds of them, all numbered and shrouded in white sheets. He and Will were supposed to keep them clean and check them once a month in case any of them suddenly became active again, but Will never bothered and Howell only did it when he got bored.

The sound of snoring drifted down the stairs. Will was asleep already. Howell felt his own eyes closing.

The door to the street rattled and opened. What was Master Tudur doing back this early? Howell sprang upright.

'Will is . . .' he began, and stopped.

The man who stepped through the door was not Master Tudur. He was tall and thin, with a long, sharp nose and a face that seemed entirely made up of straight lines.

Howell recognized him instantly. Of course he did. He'd walked past his statue less than an hour ago. He stifled a yell of fright.

Mr Bones!

He wore a crimson suit, so dark it was almost black. His trousers and jacket were closely tailored, as if he didn't want to use any more cloth than was strictly necessary, and his tall hat followed the human fashion. Mist coiled through the door after him.

People said Mr Bones could create skeletons out of the mist and if a skeleton came for you it didn't matter where you ran it would find you, and no one would ever see you again. Howell was almost sure he didn't believe a word of it, but anything was possible and he shivered and glanced about nervously.

'Are you Master Fletcher?' Mr Bones asked, removing his hat.

Howell's heart juddered. He managed to move his head enough to nod. 'Howell Fletcher. I'm the apprentice – the assistant apprentice, I mean. I keep the mirrors clean and I mind the gallery when Master Tudur isn't here. He's visiting his mother today. I could run and fetch him.' He was gabbling, his voice rising in pitch. He stopped and gulped in air. What could Mr Bones want? Master Tudur paid his taxes on time, even though he grumbled about it.

Mr Bones's gaze skimmed the room, resting on each shrouded mirror. 'Tell me, Master Fletcher, do you enjoy working here?'

Howell bit his tongue in surprise. The burst of pain annoyed him, and annoyance, he found, made him less in awe of Mr Bones. He swallowed, freeing his voice. 'I have somewhere to sleep, plenty of food and the work isn't difficult.' Why was Mr Bones asking this? Had Master Tudur complained about him? Howell reached for one of the nearby sheets. 'The mirrors are all in fine condition. I can show you.'

'No!' Mr Bones knocked Howell's hand from the sheet. His gloved hand sent a shock of cold up Howell's arm. Howell jerked back, his skin tingling.

'Thank you, but no,' Mr Bones repeated smoothly. 'I'm sure you do an excellent job.' He adjusted the sheet back over the mirror. 'I am considering appointing a new apprentice to the Mirror Station,' he said. 'Your name came recommended.'

Howell was glad he was standing by the counter because now he had to lean on it for support. His body felt hot and cold at the same time. He'd been dreaming about working at the Mirror Station only minutes ago.

'Who recommended me?' he asked. His mouth felt so dry he could barely speak.

Mr Bones ignored the question. 'A job in the Mirror

Station is a great responsibility. That is why I choose all my workers myself. I need to know that you will work hard and be trustworthy . . .'

'I will,' Howell promised. 'Master Tudur can tell you.'

'I'll speak to him in due course,' Mr Bones said. He frowned and tapped his fingers on the counter, right next to Howell's outspread hands. 'I must admit you are younger than I'd expected.'

A few moments ago, Howell had been petrified to be in the same space as Mr Bones. Now he felt a flood of hot panic that Mr Bones would leave and forget all about him.

'I work hard,' he said, 'and I'm trustworthy. If you tell me to do something, I'll do it – I promise.'

Mr Bones shook his head slightly and put his hat back on. 'Good day, Master Fletcher.'

Howell's heart sank. But then Mr Bones paused at the door. 'Maybe there is something,' he said, turning back. 'I'm sure you heard of an incident at the Mirror Station last week.'

'The anti-humanist league.' Everyone in Wyse had heard about it. The anti-humanist league had tried to break into the Station – yet another attempt to smash the last few working mirrors, and with them the covenant with the human world.

Mr Bones nodded. 'One of their members is giving us particular trouble at the moment. A young lady with pink hair and a large hat. Maybe you've seen her?'

A lady with a large hat had bumped into him outside the Mirror Station today. What colour had her hair been? Howell couldn't remember – his brain refused to work.

'I don't know,' he said. If he made a mistake and Mr Bones wasted his time chasing the wrong person, he could say farewell to any chance of working in the Mirror Station.

Mr Bones stared at him a moment longer. 'If you do see this woman, if she tries to speak to you – *especially* if she tries to speak to you – report it to me at the Mirror Station right away. Can I trust you to do that?'

A chance to prove himself trustworthy.

'Yes, of course,' Howell said.

'Good. Then I shall bid you good day for now. Naturally, it would be best if you didn't mention this conversation to anyone. If your master finds out you're considering leaving before the end of your apprenticeship, he may not pleased. He may even refuse to release you.'

He went out, letting go of the door too soon, so it slammed shut behind him. Howell jumped at the sound, then sagged back against the counter, his legs trembling, heart pounding.

That had really happened. Mr Bones – *the* Mr

Bones – was considering him for a job at the Mirror Station. He'd have to start at the bottom, no doubt, but he could work his way up, maybe even become a guard or a mirror operator. He'd outrank Will – Will wouldn't be happy about that. Howell grinned, thinking about the look on his fellow apprentice's face when he told him.

Then his grin faded and he sat back down and pushed up his sleeve to rub the round mark on his left arm. It didn't usually bother him, but all of a sudden it was itching.

Mr Bones had just walked in here and offered him the very thing he wanted. For once, everything had gone right, so why did Howell feel that something was wrong?

CHAPTER 4

Wyse, 1852. Population: 8,300. Number of visitors: 800–1,000 per week. Number of magic mirrors: 6. Those are the official numbers. The actual numbers may vary. You have been warned.

The Book

The church in Wyse seemed to be one of the few buildings in town that wasn't covered with fairy enchantments. As Ava and Matthew slipped into a wooden pew the next morning, Ava enjoyed the feeling of solidity from the old stone walls. Almost everyone turned to stare at them. Quite a few people shimmered with fairy enchantments, Ava noticed. Lord Skinner sat at the front with a whole pew to himself. He gave Matthew a friendly nod.

A fine gentle— Ava thought, and stopped herself.

The sermon was something to do with welcoming strangers and the reverend threw frequent glances at Ava and Matthew, which didn't help Ava feel any more welcome at all.

At the end of the service, people streamed out past them.

'Welcome to Wyse,' the reverend said, shaking hands with Matthew at the church doors. 'My condolences for your loss.'

Ava wondered how long it would be before people stopped saying that. One year? Two? . . . Fifty? Maybe one day she'd be an old lady and people would still greet her with a sad smile, a slight shake of the head and a 'condolences for your loss'.

'Thank you,' she replied. 'We enjoyed your sermon.'

The reverend's mouth twitched and Ava wondered if he'd noticed she'd been half asleep. He met her gaze properly, which she liked.

'I'm Reverend Stowe. I'm new in Wyse myself – six years last Easter. How are you settling in?'

'Fine,' Matthew said. 'Everyone is, um . . .'

'You'll find that people are very welcoming once you get to know them,' Reverend Stowe said. 'Give it a week or two and I'm sure you'll feel properly at home here.'

Ava doubted that. Looking around, she caught sight of Charles Brunel from the bakery. He was with two grown-ups who must have been his parents, and two older girls – sisters, probably. They had the same brown hair and round features.

'The Brunel family,' Reverend Stowe said. 'Charles

is about your age, I believe. They do some good work in Wyse.'

'Freedom for Fair Folk, I know.' Ava turned back to address the reverend. 'What do you think about magic?'

'Ava,' Matthew murmured, but Reverend Stowe smiled.

'As a matter of fact, I belong to Freedom for Fair Folk with the Brunels. The Fair Folk are people too and they deserve fair treatment. I hear you're going to be working for Lord Skinner, Mr Harcourt. You're lucky – he's a fine gentleman.'

Those words again. 'How long has Lord Skinner lived in Wyse?' Ava asked innocently.

Reverend Stowe's smile took on a slightly bemused air. 'You know, I can't really say – longer than me, that's for sure. A fine gentleman, as I said. He even helps our little protest movement, though his hands are tied for the most part. A man in his position can't be seen to show favouritism.' He sighed. 'At least today is a day of rest. No orders going through the mirrors, so the Fair Folk will have their chance to rest too.'

'Have you ever seen a fairy, Reverend Stowe?' Ava asked, but Matthew was already pushing her on.

They emerged from the church under an overcast sky. The gravestones in the grounds around the church cast pale shadows.

'I was going to ask him about the Footers,' Ava said.

'I think you asked enough questions for one conversation.'

'And I don't think I asked nearly enough.' Ava stopped in the middle of the path. 'Why don't you want to talk about fairy magic? If it's just a bit of fun, what's the problem?'

Matthew avoided her gaze. 'There *is* no problem. Look, there are the Footers.' He drew Ava in the direction of an old woman and a much younger man coming out of the church. 'Aunt Lily. Edmund. Good morning. It's been a long time. This is Ava.'

So these were the relatives who'd bought Father's magic mirror. Ava couldn't see any family resemblance at all. Father had been a quiet, small man. Edmund Footer was much taller, and Mrs Footer, though small, looked fierce with her dark eyes and tight bun of grey hair.

'We know who the girl is,' Lily Footer snapped. She stared hard at Ava and sniffed. 'She looks normal enough, I suppose.'

What had they thought she'd look like? Ava pushed back the brim of her bonnet and put on her hardest, brightest smile. 'Good morning. I'm looking forward to working for you.'

'We don't discuss work on a Sunday,' her aunt said quickly. 'We will see you tomorrow morning. Don't be late. Come along, Edmund.'

Edmund Footer shrugged apologetically as he followed his mother away.

Ava kicked the path. 'What's their problem?'

'It's not your fault,' Matthew said. 'Aunt Lily and Father never really got on. It's probably because she's so much older. And she was widowed and had to raise Edmund by herself.'

That didn't mean she had to be horrible. Ava suddenly hated this place. She hated the fake-looking enchantments and the unwelcoming people. She hated that her parents were gone and, like it or not, that this was her home now.

Matthew heaved a sigh, but then he offered Ava his arm. 'I was thinking we could take a look at those trees in the garden this afternoon. Can you remember how to climb one?'

A ray of sun broke through the clouds overhead. Ava tucked her hand through Matthew's arm and walked on. Maybe not *everything* had changed.

Of course, the neighbours on both sides of them *would* decide to pay a visit exactly when Ava was halfway up a tree.

They stood in a group, frowning at her: two men, two ladies and a gaggle of children of various ages, all looking slightly horrified. One of the children started to giggle.

'Would you like some tea?' Matthew offered.

'We can see you're busy,' one of the ladies said. 'We won't keep you. If you need anything, please, um . . .'

Please don't ask us, she meant, Ava thought. She scrambled down the tree, catching her skirt on a branch and displaying her legs right up to the knees.

The lady started to steer her children away. 'Welcome to Wyse. It's nice to see that you are well.'

'Come again soon,' Ava called after them, making them walk faster.

She waited until they were out of sight, then she rounded on Matthew. 'It's like they think there's something wrong with me.'

'Nothing's wrong with you,' Matthew said.

'Those people obviously think there is.' She watched the retreating neighbours. 'If you don't tell me, I'll just keep asking. Charles Brunel said I almost died of the measles.'

'The boy from the church? When were you talking to him?'

'In the baker's shop. Is it true?'

Matthew sighed. 'I don't know. You were very sick. But I was, what, ten years old? No one told me anything.' He shrugged uncomfortably. 'You got better, which is all that matters.'

'But?' Ava persisted. 'Matthew, come on! Tell me.'

He scuffed a foot on the ground. 'You know what people are like for gossiping, and Father was a conjuror, after all. Some people started saying he'd used magic to cure you. Especially as you were left with that mark on your face. You know what people are like with nonsense about fairy marks.'

'I thought fairy magic was only illusion. It can't *cure* people – and it can't leave marks behind.'

'It can't – but that doesn't stop people talking.' He pushed his hands into his pockets, hunching his shoulders. 'I think that's one of the reasons Father decided to leave Wyse: he was sick of the gossip.'

'And what were the other reasons he decided to leave?' Ava asked.

Matthew sighed. 'Weren't we going to make tea?'

Fine, don't tell me then. Ava stamped into the house. A crumpled piece of paper on the kitchen table caught her attention – the Freedom for Fair Folk leaflet that Charles Brunel had given her. Ava straightened it out and read:

Who do you think the Fair Folk are?
Some say they are merely illusions or
reflections, living inside the magic mirrors,
waiting to do our bidding. What do you think?

CHAPTER 5

Being a magic book of prophecy is fun sometimes, especially when you get to eavesdrop on conversations.

This one is happening right now:

'You have the girl, I hear.'

'Yes, I have her. You are not to touch her – she's mine.'

'You don't even know what she can do. For all you know, she's entirely ordinary.'

'You're just saying that because you want me to give up. You're too late: I've got her. Now, tell me about the boy.'

Interesting, isn't it?

The Book

'Are you sure you don't want me to come in with you?' Matthew asked, pausing outside the Footers' house.

Ava shaded her eyes, gazing up at the high roof. The whole house shone in various jewel-like colours and the roof was pure gold. The colours blurred as she stared, merging into one another in a dizzying fashion.

She couldn't make out the door for a moment, then she spotted it, half hidden in a tangle of red roses that shimmered and vanished as she put her hand on the gate.

'I'll be fine,' she said. She didn't want to be escorted to her first job like a child.

She waited to make sure Matthew was really going before she opened the gate. And then she waited a moment more because her heart was suddenly beating much too fast. It would be fine, she reminded herself firmly. Whatever their family history, the Footers were still family, and they'd offered her a job, hadn't they? They wouldn't have done that if they didn't want her.

She walked up the path and rang the brass bell that hung beside the door. For a few seconds nothing happened, then the door jerked open so fast Ava almost fell inside.

Lily Footer scowled out at her. 'You're early.' Her gaze fixed on the crescent on Ava's cheek, then she seemed to realize she was staring rudely and she turned away. 'Come on in, then.'

Ava stepped inside. The hallway was wide, the walls enchanted to look like gold leaf. She hadn't expected to recognize anything about the house, but even so she was disappointed to find it so unfamiliar.

'Good morning, Aunt Lily,' she said. The words felt strange – strange to think she had an aunt here at all.

'Matthew sends his greetings. He would have come, but he's due at Waning Crescent.'

Lily Footer looked her up and down. 'You can call me Mrs Footer.' She didn't speak; she barked. 'I prefer not to become over-familiar with my staff. We took you on because Lord Skinner asked and my son didn't have the wit to refuse. Don't think because we are related you can walk in as if you own the place.'

Ava stood, staring at her in shock, all her rehearsed conversation dying on her tongue. 'I didn't, I—'

Mrs Footer cut her off. 'I hope you learn quickly.'

She strode off down the hallway. Ava hurried to follow. So much for thinking everything would be fine here.

Mrs Footer opened a door and ushered Ava into the kitchen. 'You'll be responsible for keeping all the downstairs rooms clean and tidy.' She snatched at cupboard doors as she spoke, allowing Ava brief glimpses of cloths, towels and brushes. Everything she did was in a hurry, as if she was afraid of wasting a single second. 'The cook comes in mid-morning. You're to stay out of her way unless she needs you for anything, in which case she'll tell you. Mondays are laundry days. I have a girl who comes in just for that and you'll assist her.' She opened a door at the far end of the kitchen. 'You can leave your things in here. Be quick.'

The room appeared to be a combination of a

laundry room and a pantry, with jars of flour and sugar on the shelves and baskets of crumpled linen on the floor. Ava put her bonnet on the only chair and shrugged her coat off, shivering at the cold thread of air that came through the gap under the window. She'd chosen a plain grey dress to wear. She should still be in mourning, but her heavy black clothes hadn't felt appropriate for work.

'You'll need an apron,' Mrs Footer said. 'And you should cover your head. I don't want your hairs all over my house.'

As if she was planning to leave hair and mess in every room! Ava scraped her hair back with her fingers. 'I'm sorry. I'll bring an apron and headscarf tomorrow.'

'You make sure you do. Come along.'

She led the way back through the house, opening doors on to rooms and snapping instructions. A dining room contained a table that must be polished every day and never scratched. A sitting room and a small parlour had fires that must be tended and Ava must never allow a speck of soot to escape on to the rugs.

There was no sign of Father's magic mirror, though. Ava wondered where Mr Footer kept it.

Mrs Footer paused in the hallway outside the final door. 'This room is the most important one,' she said.

Ava's heart skipped. 'Is it the conjuring room?'

Mrs Footer scowled at her. 'Don't be silly, girl. Mr Footer's audience room is upstairs and it is private. *This* is my parlour where I entertain friends. I expect it to remain perfect. You will clean it every day.'

She opened the door. Ava lifted her skirt and stepped carefully, in case she accidentally dirtied anything just by being there.

The room was bigger than all the others and the morning sunshine streamed through the front windows. A marble fireplace took up most of one wall, and sofas and chairs stood around it. But Ava's gaze was drawn to the mirror that hung on the wall between the two windows, tall and narrow in an ornate silver frame.

It looked like it could be a magic mirror, though surely the Footers wouldn't leave one hanging on the wall in full view?

'Lord Skinner gave us that mirror,' Mrs Footer said. 'It came from Waning Crescent.' She paused, and even smiled thinly, waiting for Ava to be impressed.

Ava remembered seeing the patch of rearranged mirrors on the wall at Waning Crescent. No wonder this one looked like a magic mirror – once upon a time it had been. And now it was just for show, like all the fairy enchantments around the town. Mrs Footer wanted people to ask about it so she could boast about Lord Skinner giving them gifts.

'It's, um, very nice,' Ava said. 'Very reflecting.'

Mrs Footer's lips tightened back into a scowl. 'You need to get to work. Your hours will be eight in the morning until six in the evening. The cook will provide you with lunch, which you will eat in the kitchen once everyone else has eaten. You will have Sundays off, and Wednesday afternoons. I expect you to be on time, to work hard and to stay out of the way. Mr Footer is a very important man and you are not to disturb him.'

Stay out of the way, don't ask questions, never forget you aren't wanted here. Ava went back to the kitchen and found a bucket and cloth. She breathed a sigh of relief when Mrs Footer finally stopped watching her and walked away.

She hoped Matthew was having a better day than her.

'It was ghastly,' Matthew said.

He slumped in a chair in front of the fire. 'First of all, Lord Skinner didn't seem to know what to do with me, and then he told me I should catalogue all the books in his office. I spent the whole afternoon climbing up and down ladders, dragging books off shelves, writing down their titles and putting them back. My legs have never ached so badly. And you know the worst thing? It's completely pointless. When I was looking for a book to write in, I found an index of everything in the office. It was only made last year.'

'Did you tell Lord Skinner?' Ava asked.

'I did, and he said he wanted a new index – "in case anything has changed."' Matthew heaved a sigh. 'Also, the place is freezing, and there's not another soul working there that I can see. I spent the whole day shivering in my coat on my own. I hope Lord Skinner finds some real work for me soon because at the moment I'm wondering why he wanted me at all.' He groaned and stretched. 'At least he gave me a decent lunch – steak pie. He's invited us both to dinner with him again tomorrow evening, by the way.'

Again? 'Maybe he's fattening us up to eat us,' Ava said. 'You've seen the size of him.'

'Ava!'

'Sorry.' Ava rubbed her palm over her sore knuckles, still red from doing the laundry. 'The Footers don't want me, either. Aunt Lily won't even admit that she's my aunt and I didn't see Edmund all day. Mrs Footer told me they only agreed to take me on because Lord Skinner asked them. I really don't know why he bothered.'

'Maybe he acted out of kindness. He seems very pleasant.'

Seems. Ava slapped the arm of her chair, raising a cloud of dust. 'Everything *seems* in this town. Why can't things just be the way they're supposed to be?'

'This *is* how things are,' Mathew said. 'It might not be what we want, but we're stuck with it for now. I'm sure things will get better in time.'

How much time? Ava wondered. *A month? A year?* She was pretty sure Mrs Footer was never going to like her and, as for this town with its gossip and secrets, Ava was beginning to think she'd rather be back in Cambridge and homeless.

CHAPTER 6

The covenant says magic mirrors are doors between the two worlds. Not literal doors, of course. Doors require no special magic to use them. When you look into a magic mirror, your reflection appears in its partner mirror. Then you simply put yourself into your reflection and step out. It takes a touch of magic to achieve, which is why few humans can do it, and you must be invited by someone on the other side because we can't have people wandering between worlds willy-nilly. That would cause all sorts of trouble – though no worse than the trouble that's coming.

The Book

Five days had passed since Mr Bones first came into the House of Forgotten Mirrors. He'd been back twice since, once to check if Howell had seen any sign of the pink-haired lady, and another time because he said he just happened to be passing. And today . . .

'No, I still haven't seen the anti-humanist lady,' Howell said. 'I'm sorry. I've looked for her every time I've gone outside.'

Mr Bones frowned and stared at him hard, as if trying to decide whether to believe him. 'Keep looking,' he said finally. 'If she's still in Unwyse, you'll run into her.'

He seemed very sure of that. Howell wondered why. He opened his mouth to ask, but Mr Bones picked Howell's coat off the stand and tossed it to him.

'I thought you might like to visit the Mirror Station today,' he said casually.

Howell missed his coat and it slid to the floor. 'What, now?'

'Why not? Your master won't be back until evening, and your fellow apprentice . . .'

Was upstairs sleeping off lunch. How did Mr Bones know where everyone was? Howell picked up his coat off the floor. He could shut the gallery for an hour; nobody would know.

His heart raced as he followed Mr Bones outside. The afternoon was bright with folds of yellow and orange mist trailing along the ground. Fist-sized pieces of it broke off as Mr Bones walked through it and attached to his coat, hanging there like baubles. Howell watched it in fascination. He'd never seen mist behave like this before. The stories he'd heard about Mr Bones creating skeleton servants out of mist seemed even more believable, and he felt a shiver go through him.

'Does it always do that?' he asked, edging away.

Mr Bones shook his coat, dislodging bits of clinging orange. 'Sometimes. Don't dawdle, boy.'

He walked through the crowds outside the Mirror Station as if they weren't there, and, somehow, they weren't. People scrambled to get out of his way, touching their hats respectfully or even bowing. A few people bumped into Howell, too busy staring after Mr Bones to notice he was there, but Howell didn't care. He was here with Mr Bones, he thought, and for a moment a swell of pride chased all other thoughts out of his head.

Mr Bones, ruler of Unwyse. When the mirrors were failing all over the Unworld, he'd set up the Mirror Station and brought the last few working mirrors here, and somehow – Howell didn't quite know how – he'd kept them working. He'd set up Waxing Gibbous to supply enchantments to the humans and kept things running ever since. And now he was thinking of offering Howell a job.

Seconds later, they were walking into the Station itself where porters in red uniforms were checking labels on boxes. Everyone stood up straight when they saw Mr Bones.

'Continue as you were,' Mr Bones said. 'Master Fletcher, this way.'

Then he paused, frowning as if he'd just noticed something. 'I must attend to an urgent matter,' he said. He caught hold of a nearby guard. 'Show this boy around the station. Let him watch the mirrors for a while. We will speak again later, Master Fletcher.' He strode away and ducked through a door, seeming to vanish a second before the door closed.

The guard turned to Howell. 'He does this all the time,' he said. 'He's probably been called to the factory – he has a direct access hatch for emergencies.'

'A what?'

'A magical shortcut. I think – I've never actually seen it myself.' He smiled thinly. 'I'm Luel. Come on. I'll show you the mirrors.'

Howell had spent the past three months surrounded by mirrors, but he'd never seen a working one before. The six mirrors stood in a line, with silver curtains dividing them. The six mirror operators sat in a row in front, some reading, others knitting or sewing.

'Impressed?' Luel asked.

Howell nodded because Luel seemed to expect it. In fact, he was thinking how ordinary it all looked.

Then one of the mirrors turned misty and Howell stopped thinking altogether. The operator sat up straight, shoving her knitting under her stool. Luel pulled Howell back as the glass cleared to show, not the operator's reflection, but a human man – young and plump with hair like dried grass and a thick brown moustache.

'Stay at the side where he can't see you,' Luel

whispered. 'The humans like to think they're getting personal service. If they knew there were loads of us here it'd spoil the magic for them.'

'The magic?' Howell queried.

'Of course. We need to make it look good. Most of what we send them is all about appearance.'

The operator took out a silver notebook. 'Greetings from the Unworld, Mr Footer. We await your orders.'

The human opened up a notebook of his own. 'One hundred enchanted roses,' he read. 'Sixteen full tea sets. Twenty gowns to make the wearer appear more beautiful.' He sounded bored.

The operator scribbled furiously as the human read through the list. 'To be delivered on Monday morning,' he said. 'That is all.'

The mirror clouded, then cleared to show the operator's own reflection again. She sighed, tore the page out of the notebook and dropped it into a basket.

'Is that it?' Howell asked.

Luel was already turning away. 'Pretty much. Someone will gather up the orders later and send them through to Waxing Gibbous. They'll box the goods up and bring them here to be delivered through the mirror on Monday. Sometimes the humans will ask for something we haven't got at the factory and we'll have to order it in from the town, and sometimes they ask us questions. As if we know the answers to anything about *their* world! Mostly it's just orders, though. The main part of my job, besides guard duty, is making sure goods are sent through the correct mirror.'

'Have you ever been through a mirror?' Howell asked. 'All the way into the human world, I mean?'

Luel laughed and shook his head. 'That would be something, wouldn't it? But I don't remember the last time anyone went through. Humans are happy enough taking our enchantments, less happy with letting us into their world.'

'What about Mr Bones?' Howell asked. Surely Mr Bones must have seen the human world. But Luel shook his head again.

'I've never even seen Mr Bones look at a mirror. It really is just a case of taking orders from humans.'

'Oh.' Somehow, Howell had imagined life at the Mirror Station would be more exciting than this. No wonder Master Tudur complained about his taxes being wasted. 'What about the anti-humanists? I heard they were causing trouble.'

'They do, now and then. Mainly they just stand outside and shout and we ignore them.' He tugged his jacket straight importantly. 'Don't tell Mr Bones I told you this, but everyone here thinks these mirrors are going to die one day – with or without the anti-humanists' help. All the others have, haven't they? And, when these ones do, it won't matter about the covenant with their world – the humans won't be able to make any more demands of us.'

Howell's jaw dropped. 'But, if there are no mirrors . . .' He tailed off. That would mean no Mirror Station, no Waxing Gibbous, no need for Mr Bones. Howell swallowed nervously. 'What do you think of Mr Bones?' he asked. 'Do you like him?'

Something in Luel's expression froze: a quick look of fear, just as quickly banished. 'He's fine,' he said. 'A gentleman.' He glanced over his shoulder as if he expected Mr Bones to appear behind him there and then. 'Stay on the right side of him and you'll do well.'

And if he strayed on to the wrong side? Howell nodded. 'I ought to get back before I'm missed.' The words felt thick in his mouth. 'Thanks for showing me around.'

He cast a last look back at the mirrors. Another one was turning misty, the operator opening a notepad in readiness.

Howell left the Mirror Station in a daze. Six working mirrors, keeping the whole great factory of Waxing Gibbous running. It seemed a precariously small number all of a sudden. Their connection with the human world was hanging by a thread and nobody seemed to question it. Or perhaps they were afraid to.

He began to shove his way through the crowds. No one got out of his way now. A few people shouted at him as he squeezed past.

Then a hand caught his arm. 'Howell, remember number seventy-seven,' a voice said.

Howell turned and let out a yelp of panic. It was the lady with pink hair – the anti-humanist! She didn't look dangerous. She was quite young and her hair made Howell think of strawberry pie.

Howell backed away rapidly. 'How do you know my name?' Where was Mr Bones? He needed to report this.

The anti-humanist shook her head. 'You're in grave danger. Don't trust Mr Bones and remember number seventy-seven.'

Then she was gone, disappearing into the crowded square.

Howell stood, his feet stuck to the spot. Why would an anti-humanist risk coming to the Mirror Station to warn him?

Someone elbowed him. 'Sorry,' Howell said, and moved aside. Then, because he couldn't decide what to do next, he made his way home.

The House of Forgotten Mirrors was empty. Good – the last thing Howell wanted was questions from Master Tudur or Will about where he'd gone. He fetched a cloth and polish, and started to clean the mirrors, his face creased in a troubled frown. He wished he knew what to think.

Remember number seventy-seven.

It was only a number. It could mean anything, or nothing at all. But, leaving the mirror he was cleaning, Howell strode across the gallery and jerked the sheet off number seventy-seven.

The glass showed only his own face and the gallery behind him. All perfectly normal. Howell laughed shakily, his breath misting the mirror, and began wiping the glass down.

For some reason, the patch of mist where he'd breathed on the glass didn't clear – instead it seemed to be spreading. Howell rubbed it harder.

Then, in a blink, the mirror cleared. The cloth fell from Howell's hand, forgotten.

In a glass that had never done anything but reflect Howell's own face, he saw a different face. A girl, with dark hair escaping from a grey headscarf and a mark on her cheek like the setting moon.

CHAPTER 7

Britain in 1852 no longer needs magic. Britain rules the waves very nicely without it. Industry is the new magic: factories and machines and engines. What's the point of a fairy enchantment that fades when you can have something made that will last for years?

It's a sad world that has outgrown its need for magic, but what do I know? As I think I might have mentioned, I'm only a book.

The Book

Ava had been cleaning the front parlour, glad the day was almost over, glad it was Saturday and so she'd have tomorrow off. This week felt like it had gone on forever. Mrs Footer snapping at her all day long, and Lord Skinner watching her each night over the dining table.

He's a fine gentleman.

The words slid into her head and Ava shook them away. She looked up and caught her reflection in the long mirror and her heart sank a little lower. She seemed like a different person with her grey dress and white apron, her hair tucked up into a cotton headscarf. Only the mark on her cheek remained the same.

Ava walked defiantly to the mirror. She wasn't going to clean houses forever. She was more than just a housemaid, whatever the Footers thought of her. Her reflection turned misty where her breath clouded the glass.

Poor mirror, Ava thought. It should be a doorway to the Unworld. Instead, it hung all alone with nothing to do but impress Mrs Footer's horrible friends.

The patch of mist on the glass spread. Then, before Ava could react, the mirror cleared and she wasn't looking at her reflection any more. A boy stared out of the mirror at her. A boy with green hair and pointed ears, and eyes with enormous, dark pupils, looking completely terrified.

Ava froze. She could hear the cook still clattering pans in the kitchen. People walked past on the street outside, their voices drifting into the room. The world carried on exactly the same around her while, impossibly, a fairy boy stared back at her from behind a mirror.

If he didn't blink, his eyes were going to get stuck, Ava thought, and she realized that she hadn't blinked all this time either. She drew in a breath and shut her eyes briefly, afraid he'd vanish the moment she stopped looking at him.

He was still there. Ava smiled tentatively, her heart hammering. 'Hello?' Could he even hear her?

The boy made up for all the staring by blinking rapidly several times. 'Uh, hello.'

That answered her question. Ava wasn't sure what to say next.

'Are you a fairy?' she asked. Stupid. Of course he was.

The fairy boy flashed a frown. 'No. I'm one of the Fair Folk. How would you like it if we called you humanies?'

It wasn't particularly funny, but Ava had the urge to giggle. 'I suppose I wouldn't like it. Sorry.' She glanced back at the door to make sure it was shut. The last thing she wanted was Mrs Footer walking in on her now.

The boy turned and looked behind him as if he, too, was checking he was alone. 'This shouldn't be happening,' he said. 'This mirror hasn't worked for a hundred years. Something very strange is going on.'

'Yes, I'd noticed.' Ava touched the edge of the mirror frame, afraid that whatever magic had made the mirror work would disappear just as suddenly. 'I'm Ava Harcourt. From Wyse.'

'Howell Fletcher from Unwyse,' the boy said, tugging at a stray thread on his shirt. 'How did you make the mirror work?'

'I didn't. I was just looking at it.' Ava rubbed her hand across her cheek. 'You must have done something.'

'Me? I was just cleaning it. I don't suppose you've seen a lady in a big hat, have you? Or Mr Bones?'

Ava shook her head. 'Who is Mr Bones?'

Howell blinked a few extra times. 'You don't know Mr Bones? He rules Unwyse. He owns the Mirror Station and Waxing Gibbous. Everyone knows him.'

Ava wondered what the Mirror Station and Waxing Gibbous were. 'Everyone on your side of the mirror knows him, maybe,' she said. 'But not here.' She tried to remember what was written in the Freedom for Fair Folk leaflet Charles had given her. 'Is Unwyse an actual, real place? You don't live in the mirrors, like reflections?'

Now Howell looked at her as if he thought she was mad. 'You do know that reflections aren't alive, right? Otherwise they'd be able to move around and talk back to you.'

Ava felt a flush crawl up her face. 'There's no need to be rude. How am I supposed to know how mirrors work? I'm not a conjuror.'

'Sorry,' Howell said, but his lips twitched with laughter. He ran a hand through his hair. 'Magic mirrors act as doors between our worlds. The mirrors on your side open into our Mirror Station and the mirror operators take your orders, which are fulfilled at Waxing Gibbous. And mirrors that don't work are stored in the House of Forgotten Mirrors, which is where I am now.'

Ava didn't want to admit she had no idea what he was talking about. 'I'm in my cousin's house,' she said. 'He's the conjuror, but this isn't the mirror he uses. I'm not sure he really understands much about magic.'

Howell scratched behind one pointed ear. 'As I said, something very strange is happening.'

Lord Skinner. Ava knew there was something odd about him. He had placed Ava with the Footers; he'd given them the mirror. Could he be behind this?

'I think . . .' Ava began, and broke off as a door opened in the hallway and she heard Mrs Footer barking her name. Ava groaned. 'I have to go. Can we talk again?'

'I suppose, if the mirror works. Tomorrow?'

Ava almost nodded and caught herself. Tomorrow was Sunday. 'Monday,' she said. 'I'll be here between five and six o'clock. Is that the same time in Unwyse?'

'It's nearly six here now, so I guess so. I'll watch for you.'

'Don't tell anyone,' Ava added. If word got back to the Footers, they'd never let her near the mirror again.

'See you Monday,' Howell said. He bent and picked up a sheet from the floor on his side of the mirror. For a second he held it, then he reached up with it and the glass turned white as he draped it over. A moment later, the mirror cleared and showed Ava's own reflection again. Her cheeks were pink, the crescent-shaped mark standing out sharply.

Where's your sense of adventure, Ava?

She opened the door and stepped out into the hall. 'Mrs Footer,' she said, 'I was wondering about your new mirror. When did Lord Skinner give it to you?'

'A few weeks ago. He offered it to us as thanks for taking you, and just as well he did as you've not proved worth your wages so far. Go and help in the kitchen if you've finished cleaning.'

She didn't know the mirror was working, Ava thought, and just for a moment relief flooded her. She cast a final look back at the mirror as she left the room.

Stay away from mirrors. Don't trust Lord Skinner. He's not what he seems.

The truth is in the detail.

Something very strange is going on.

The thoughts kept circling Ava's mind until it was time to leave the Footers' house.

Ava knew she should go straight home after work, but she needed time to think and the evening was bright. She walked into the town centre and wandered slowly, studying the various enchantments on the buildings. She could see where some of them were fading and turning patchy, revealing the red brick underneath. Lamps started to come on along the road by the theatre, globes of enchanted light, some of them shining brightly, others dull, streaked with dirty brown.

'That's the problem with fairy magic,' a boy's voice said. 'It doesn't last.'

Ava turned to see Charles Brunel holding an empty bread basket. 'Gas would be far better,' he said, nodding at a lamp. 'It's clean, it's easy and you don't need to make people work for nothing. Nice to see you again, by the way.'

Ava nodded, though she wasn't sure whether she was pleased to see him or not. She didn't much feel like talking to anyone right now. On the other hand, Charles probably knew as much about Fair Folk as anyone in Wyse.

'Why do the Fair Folk work for nothing?' she asked. 'Couldn't they just say no?'

'For a conjuror's daughter, you really don't know a lot about magic, do you? It's because of the covenant.'

Ava almost retorted that her father hadn't talked much about magic, and now he'd passed away so she could hardly ask him. But none of that was Charles's fault. She paused, then asked: 'What's the covenant?'

Charles set his basket down and wiped his hands on his trousers. 'There's an old story that the Fair

Folk used to live here, in our world, but one day they left, and they took all the magic with them. But, as a parting gift, they gave us the mirrors and they made a covenant with us that we could access their magic when we needed it. Only, instead of keeping it for when we really needed magic, we started demanding enchantments and charms and treating the Fair Folk like slaves. That might even be why the mirrors stopped working – we misused them.'

Ava thought of Howell, gazing back at her through a mirror that shouldn't be working. She almost blurted it out.

'It's only a story,' Charles said. 'It might be completely made up for all I know.'

Something about it felt right, though, as if Ava had heard the story many times before. Maybe her father used to tell it to her.

'How are you getting on with the Footers?' Charles asked. 'Not very well, I'd guess.'

Ava tucked a strand of hair back inside her bonnet. 'What makes you think that?'

Charles gestured to her hands. 'You're covered in dust. You didn't even take a minute to wash before leaving. That suggests you couldn't wait to escape.' He grinned. 'And, also, Mrs Footer is horrible. Some people say her husband died just to get away from her.' His smile quickly faded. 'I'm sorry. That was thoughtless.'

'Why? Because my parents died?' At least he wasn't trying to pretend it hadn't happened. Ava glanced back up at the failing street lamp. Its light was almost all brown now and she could make out the shape of leaves inside the glass globe. If Mrs Footer caught her talking to a boy in the street, she'd probably sack her on the spot, but Ava didn't care. 'Tell me more about the covenant,' she said. 'What happens if it breaks?'

'All the magic comes back here and the Unworld ends. Or something like that.' Charles bent to pick his basket up. 'You should come to the Freedom for Fair Folk meeting. Every Thursday at number two Church Street. You can come for tea first, if you like.'

His smile was hopeful and Ava got the impression that Freedom for Fair Folk rarely got new members.

'Thanks,' she said. 'I'll think about it.'

'And if you need help with anything just come and ask,' Charles said. 'If the Footers get too much for you, or you want to know anything else about Lord Skinner. What did you think of him?'

He's a fine gentleman. The words were right there in her head.

'I'm not sure,' she said slowly. 'He's . . . odd.'

'Told you.' Charles nodded eagerly. 'Did you notice the smell? No one else seems to.'

Ava nodded. 'Like damp leaves and mouldy bread.' She shuddered, remembering. 'Matthew likes him, although he says he doesn't know why Lord Skinner employed him as there's hardly any work to do. And I found out Lord Skinner gave the Footers a mirror from Waning Crescent in return for them giving me a job.' It didn't sound terribly suspicious, put like that. She expected Charles to laugh at her, but he dug out his notebook instead and scribbled in it.

'It could be charity – we shouldn't rule out the obvious. But we should keep gathering clues.'

He seemed to assume Ava would agree, as if she'd become his detective assistant all of a sudden. She was beginning to suspect that, not only did Freedom for Fair Folk lack members, but Charles lacked friends.

Charles slung his basket over his arm. 'I'd better get home. See you soon. You can find me at Church Street if you need me, or in the bakery.'

He walked away, whistling. Ava watched him go, her frown growing deeper. She was already beginning to wish she hadn't mentioned the mirror to Charles. He was a boy who loved mysteries. How long would it take him to uncover her secret?

CHAPTER 8

Look, the thing about predicting the future is this: it's hard. So much of the future depends on what has happened previously. All I can say for sure is we are in a lot of trouble. Probably a 77 per cent chance of us all being doomed, but who knows?

The Book

Howell smoothed the sheet down over the mirror and walked back to Master Tudur's chair on shaky legs. A human girl. In a mirror that had stopped working almost a hundred years ago.

This might be a trick – a test set up by Mr Bones to see what he'd do, but somehow Howell doubted it. If Mr Bones could make mirrors work again, he'd have filled the Mirror Station with them and made himself far richer than he already was.

Howell sat for a long time, watching the shrouded mirrors until Master Tudur came in.

'Where's Will?' he asked, shaking his coat out and hanging it up.

'Upstairs.'

Master Tudur nodded and started to go on up the stairs, but then paused, turning back. 'Has something happened, Howell? You don't look quite right.'

For a moment he considered telling Master Tudur everything, but the words wouldn't come. Ava had asked him to keep this secret and, according to the covenant, he had to fulfil her request. That's what he'd say if anyone found out about this, anyway. Technically, it wasn't a magical service, so he wasn't bound, but with the covenant so fragile no one would blame him for being careful.

'Everything's fine,' he said. 'Why wouldn't it be?'

'Oh. That's good, then. Well done. You can close up now if you like.' He put a handful of pennies on the counter. 'Go and see if the bakery is still open, if you like, and don't tell Will.' He patted Howell on the shoulder, clearly thinking he was cheering him up. Howell forced a smile in return. First Mr Bones suddenly taking an interest in him, then the lady in the hat, and now Ava appearing. Howell wished he knew what to make of it all.

On Sunday morning, the mist drifted in clouds, smelling of apples. Howell went out to buy breakfast earlier than usual, hoping to avoid Mr Bones if he came looking for him, but he'd barely left the House of Forgotten Mirrors when he saw the tall figure striding towards him.

'Good morning, Master Fletcher. I trust you enjoyed your visit to the Mirror Station yesterday.'

Howell almost stumbled in relief. Mr Bones didn't know about Ava. He'd have mentioned it straight away if he did. Probably. Unless he was trying to trap him.

'It was very good, thank you,' Howell said. His head was beginning to ache, trying to keep his thoughts straight.

'Good. I'm sorry I had to leave you. Unexpected business.' Mr Bones fell into step beside him. 'I have a question.'

Howell tensed. But instead of asking about mirrors or pink-haired anti-humanists, Mr Bones waved away a patch of mist and said, 'Tell me, what do you make of the covenant?'

Howell stumbled again, this time in surprise. 'The covenant? It's . . . it's just there, isn't it? Master Tudur says it's a necessary nuisance. I know the anti-humanists would like to break it.'

'But what do you think?' Mr Bones said. 'Can you see the covenant ever changing?'

Howell had to concentrate on picking his feet up as he walked. 'I suppose if all the mirrors stop working, the covenant will end,' he said. He risked a glance at the tall figure beside him. 'Is it true that the Unworld would end with it?'

Mr Bones paused, yellow mist swirling about him. 'We made our world a mirror image of theirs,' he said. 'Can a reflection exist on its own?'

'But *we* exist on our own,' Howell protested. 'Just because the Unworld is a copy of the human world, it doesn't mean it's not real.'

'Yet, what is the Unworld?' Mr Bones said. 'A world made of magic and dreams. If the covenant ends, our magic will vanish and we will be left only with dreams.' He waved away a clump of mist. 'However, I didn't ask about the covenant ending. I asked about it changing.'

Howell gave a strangled laugh. 'You might as well try to change the worlds.'

'Exactly.' Mr Bones leaned closer, lowering his voice. 'What if we could remake the worlds – not just our own, but the human world too? What would you change?'

A patch of strawberry-pink mist drifted by, reminding Howell of the woman with the pink hair, and he felt a shiver of unease all the way down his back.

'I don't know,' he said carefully, noticing how closely Mr Bones was watching him. 'I've never really thought about it.'

Mr Bones shook his head, his thin face creasing with . . . what? Disappointment? Annoyance?

'It always pays to think about things,' he said. The

mist around him turned into skull shapes before dispersing.

Howell swallowed. Mr Bones was clearly not happy with him this morning. He rattled the coins in his pocket. 'I have to go to the bakery. Master Tudur said no dawdling.'

'Did he?' Mist curled between them. Mr Bones raised a disbelieving eyebrow and then he inclined his head. 'Off you run, then.'

For a second, Howell's feet felt as if they were glued to the road, then he was running.

The covenant? Why would Mr Bones suddenly start asking him about the covenant?

CHAPTER 9

Have you ever wondered where the term 'Fair Folk' came from? I bet you haven't. Or, if you have, you think it's because they are all fair in the Unworld. Not true. The term comes from the old word 'fere', which means 'servant'. So there.

The Book

It was Monday morning and Ava stood peering through a crack in Edmund Footer's door. She couldn't see much, but she could hear her cousin's voice droning on to a family of holidaymakers about how fairies lived in the backs of magic mirrors and were summoned into being when the conjuror uttered the magical incantations.

'But why do magic mirrors only work in Wyse?' the father of the group asked.

'Because Wyse is set on exactly the border of England and Wales,' Edmund Footer replied. 'It straddles two worlds, you see.'

Rubbish, Ava thought. *If that was true, any town on a border would have magic mirrors*. She leaned a little closer to the door as her cousin continued.

'I will now say the incantation of conjuration. You will see the mirror turn to mist and then the fairy will appear. I will place your orders just as if we're in a shop. It is quite safe.'

He raised his arms dramatically and began chanting. Ava caught a few words of Latin, but mostly it sounded made up.

A door creaked downstairs: Mrs Footer was home. Ava crept quietly back to the stairs and began sweeping them. She couldn't help feeling a bit sorry for her cousin – he had Mrs Footer for a mother, after all – but, as she'd said to Howell, he really didn't understand much about fairy magic.

Probably just as well he didn't, or he might work out that the mirror hanging downstairs in the parlour was not only magic, but active again.

'Leave those stairs alone,' Mrs Footer said. 'I don't want you disturbing Mr Footer's guests.'

Guests? Customers, more like it. Once you took away the nonsense Latin and the talk about magic, Mr Footer was just selling things. Ava stood up and wiped her hands on her apron.

'Aunt Lily, may I ask you a question?'

Mrs Footer stiffened. Ava knew she didn't like to be called 'Aunt' but Ava wanted to remind her they were family. 'Everyone says fairy magic only affects appearances,' she said. 'Is that true?'

Mrs Footer frowned. 'You'd do well to keep your questions to housekeeping matters. Your father gave up all claim to his magic mirror when he sold it to my son.'

'Yes, but . . .' Ava took a breath. 'Matthew said I almost died of measles when I was two, and some people seem to think my father cured me with magic, but that's not possible, is it?'

Mrs Footer's gaze flicked to the mark on Ava's cheek. 'No, it's not possible. Fairy magic is a wonderful thing, but it cannot change what's real. For example,' she added pointedly, 'fairy magic could make this house appear clean, but it won't really be clean unless you do your work. You can polish the candlesticks next.'

Sighing, Ava fetched a cloth. At least Mrs Footer had spoken to her, though. Maybe with time – another year or two – she might actually speak without snapping. Or maybe that was as impossible as magic changing reality.

Finally, the clock's hands crept round to five o'clock. Ava waited anxiously, wondering whether Howell would appear at all and when the mirror clouded she laughed in relief.

She'd thought Howell would be happy to see her, but he looked nervous, stepping close to the mirror and glancing around every few seconds.

'What's wrong?' Ava asked.

'Nothing. It's just . . .' Howell ran a hand through his hair. 'This whole thing is weird. If anyone finds out, I'll be in such trouble.'

He wouldn't be the only one. Ava tried to ignore the churning in her own stomach. 'Have you ever heard of Lord Skinner?' Ava asked. 'He's in charge of Wyse and everyone says he's a fine gentleman.'

'But you don't like him,' Howell said.

'I didn't say that.'

'You're thinking it, though, aren't you?' He flashed her a nervous grin, then shrugged. 'Anyway, I've never heard of him. Mr Bones is in charge here. I ought to tell him what's going on.'

'But you don't want to,' Ava said. 'You don't trust him.'

'I didn't say that.'

'You're thinking it, though.'

They both smiled.

Ava tucked her hair back behind her ears. Strange how you just instantly felt you knew certain people – stranger still when that person was from another world.

'So, what do you want to talk about?' Howell asked.

Ava considered. She had so many questions that she didn't know what to ask first. 'Unwyse,' she said eventually. 'Tell me all about Unwyse.'

*

Lord Skinner served roast chicken that evening. He ate quickly, not appearing to notice that Ava picked at her food, barely touching it.

'How do you like the Footers?' he asked.

Ava felt a blush creep up her neck. 'They're very nice.'

'Really? I always thought Mrs Footer was like a snappy little dog.'

Ava smothered a giggle. Matthew kicked her under the table.

Lord Skinner set his knife and fork down briefly. 'Has Mr Footer given you a demonstration of the magic mirror yet?'

Ava shook her head. 'He is very busy.'

'I'm sure he can find time. It was your father's mirror, after all. I'll speak to him if you wish.'

Again her vision blurred, and the smell of damp leaves surrounded her. Lord Skinner was much nicer than the Footers. She wished she could work for him.

'Do you think a broken magic mirror could ever start working again?' she asked dreamily.

Matthew sighed and rolled his eyes, but Lord Skinner leaned forward across the table. 'That's an interesting question. Why do you ask?'

Ava felt the words getting ready to spill out. She bit down on the inside of her cheek and the jolt of pain brought her vision back into focus. Her face grew warm.

'No reason. It might happen, though, mightn't it? No one knows why the mirrors stopped, so they might start working again. Suppose I looked into a mirror one day and saw an Unworld boy looking back . . .'

'An Unworld boy.' Lord Skinner pushed his plate back and a servant slipped silently to the table to collect it. 'Any particular Unworld boy?'

Ava instantly wished she'd kept her mouth shut. 'No. I don't know of any Unworld boys. I was just wondering.'

Lord Skinner watched her a moment longer, then nodded. 'It's always good to wonder.'

The servants brought in a silver trolley loaded with desserts – large bowls of trifle, a lemon tart, even a perfectly white blancmange.

'You should visit again,' Lord Skinner said, picking up a jug of cream. 'Tomorrow.'

Matthew beamed, and babbled thanks. Ava sat silently, not touching any of the desserts. They all suddenly smelled funny, as if they'd been sitting in the hot kitchen for far too long. Why had she mentioned an Unworld boy? She'd come here determined not to say a thing, then she'd started thinking Lord Skinner was a fine gentleman again and the words had just come out. What was he doing to her?

As Howell said, something very strange was going on.

CHAPTER 10

Fairy enchantments are created by drawing magic from the mist that fills the Unworld. Flimsy as the air they come from, they only affect the surface appearance of things, and they fade. But there are other kinds of magic – the old magic that links the worlds through the mirrors. And the living magic that inhabits people.

Actually, there are lots of books on this subject. If you want to know more, go and read one of them and stop bothering me. What do you think I am – an encyclopaedia?

The Book

Somehow, a whole week had gone by. Howell had moved mirror seventy-seven to the far corner of the gallery, where it was out of sight of the front desk and the doors. He hadn't seen the pink-haired lady again, but Mr Bones still called on him daily – as did Ava. Howell found himself looking forward to their conversations more and more, even though he lived under a cloud of dread that someone would find out.

The following Saturday afternoon, he sat before

the mirror, a cloth in his hand ready to jump up and pretend he was cleaning it if anyone came in.

Ava's reflection also held a cloth, and she twisted it into knots as they talked. 'Lord Skinner has invited us to dinner again. I don't want to go, but Matthew still thinks he's a fine gentleman and won't hear a word against him.'

Howell scratched the tip of an ear. 'Mr Bones has invited me back to the Mirror Station. He wants me to spend the whole day this time.'

'Are you going?'

'I don't have much choice. If I don't go, he'll know I'm trying to avoid him.'

They both sighed.

'I seem to be the only person in Unwyse who doesn't trust Mr Bones,' Howell said. 'Except for the pink-haired lady, whoever she is.'

'And I'm the only person in Wyse who doesn't think Lord Skinner is a fine gentleman. Except for Charles, and I haven't seen him all week.'

It seemed they had the same problem, Howell thought, albeit with different people. Maybe that was why he was beginning to feel closer to Ava, a human, than he did to Will or Master Tudur, who were from his own world.

'Maybe I can help,' he said cautiously. 'What if I could get you an enchantment to reveal Lord Skinner's true nature?'

Ava's eyes opened wide. 'But I thought they were illusions. They don't reveal the truth – they cover it up.'

'The ones we usually send to you do, but there are others. Things you never think to ask for.'

A thump came from upstairs. That would be Will, getting out of bed. Howell tensed.

Ava looked down at her hands. 'I don't want to get you into trouble.'

'You won't.' In fact, Howell could think of a hundred ways he'd get into trouble for this. He'd need to go to an enchantment shop, which meant he'd need money, and if word got back to Master Tudur there'd be all sorts of awkward questions.

'I'll pay,' Ava offered. 'I don't have much, but . . .'

Howell shook his head. 'There's no need. If you ask for something through a mirror, we have to do it. It's in the covenant.' And, oddly, he found that he wanted to help, despite the trouble it might cause. He wanted to know the truth too.

'Howell?' Will shouted. 'Are you downstairs?'

'I have to go,' Howell said. 'Come back later tonight – at moonrise. I'll see what I can do.' He scrambled up.

'No, wait,' Ava said.

No time. Howell pulled the sheet over the mirror, cutting off whatever she'd been trying to say.

Will clumped down into the gallery a moment later.

'Who were you talking to? Don't say you weren't – I heard you.'

'I was shouting to you, idiot, asking if you were awake.'

Will shoved him. 'Don't call me an idiot.'

'Don't act like one, then,' Howell said, shoving him back.

Surprise flashed across Will's face, and Howell was almost surprised at himself too. He didn't usually stand up to Will. He grabbed his coat from the stand by the counter. 'We're low on bread. I'm going to see if the baker has got anything.'

He had three hours, more or less, until moonrise. Where could he find an enchantment?

Howell kept away from the Mirror Station in case Mr Bones decided to come looking for him again, and headed in the opposite direction where the roads were narrower and the alleys between houses were full of rubbish.

Something scuttled behind him. He spun round, but the lane was empty. He was frightened of shadows now. Howell forced out a laugh, which didn't make him feel any less jumpy.

But then an arm shot out to block his way. Three boys emerged from a doorway. They were all about Will's age, and about his size too.

Howell stepped back, felt a tightening in his chest.

'What do you want?'

The boys looked at each other and laughed. 'We're collecting donations for the anti-humanist league. We're going to end the covenant and set the Unworld free. How much money have you got?'

Howell didn't believe the boys were really anti-humanists, but it didn't matter: they'd take every coin he had. If he was lucky, they'd shove him around a bit, then let him go. If he was unlucky, it might be worse. He put his hand in his pocket, feeling the few coins there.

The biggest boy pushed him. 'Come on. Hand it over.'

Another day, Howell might have done it. Today, however, was an odd sort of a day. He took his hands out of his pockets, looked down at them, then he punched the boy on the nose and ran.

He couldn't believe he'd just done that.

'Get him!' the boy shouted.

Feet pounded after him. Howell ran faster, tripping through piles of rubbish. He should have just given them the money. They'd have let him go before, but now they were going to beat him half to death.

A shape emerged out of the mist ahead of him and he ran straight into it. Howell bounced back and looked up to see the wide brim of a hat, striped green and blue like a tiger.

'Hello again,' the pink-haired lady said. 'Excuse

me.' She took her hat off and tossed it on the ground as the three boys came running down the alley.

In a blink, an actual, real tiger stood in front of them.

Howell yelled in fright and stumbled back. The tiger roared and the three boys screamed and fled.

'My attack hat,' the lady said, catching hold of the tiger by its green tail. Instead of eating her, it transformed back into a hat. She set it on her head and adjusted her bag on her shoulder. 'We need to talk.'

All the questions – Mr Bones, the mirror, the covenant, everything that had happened – bubbled up in a moment.

'Who are you?' Howell burst out. 'What's going on? Why are mirrors working again? *Why* shouldn't I trust Mr Bones?' He leaned against the wall; he would have sat down if there'd been anywhere to sit. 'Why is this all happening to me? I'm just an assistant apprentice. I don't even have any magic.'

'My name is Lunette,' the lady said. 'I came to warn you. You're in danger – we all are.' She fished a small packet out of her bag. 'Here: I believe you want this.'

Howell read the label in disbelief.

Madame Brille
Purveyor of Artisan Enchantments
  throughout the Unworld
77 Euphorbia Lane, Unwyse

Ingredients: fern, oak, daisy, lavender.
To reveal a person's true nature.
Warning – this item is not a toy. Handle with care.

Howell sniffed the packet suspiciously. It smelled mainly of lavender. 'You know Mad Brille?'

'She's my aunt,' Lunette said.

Howell's cheeks flared. 'Sorry. It's just that everyone says . . .'

'She's odd, I know. She's very nice, though, when you get to know her. She made that enchantment as soon as I told her you'd want it.'

But he'd only talked to Ava a few minutes ago, Howell thought. There was no way Lunette could have known.

The hat-wielding niece of the madwoman glanced about. 'Would you mind if we get out of the cold? There's a teashop nearby. I can explain everything there.'

She appeared so sure Howell would say yes that he found himself nodding. Although, come to think of it, explanations would be pretty good right now.

'My master is expecting me back,' he said as he followed Lunette back down the lane, just to let her know that he'd be missed if he didn't return. 'Who told you I wanted that enchantment?'

Lunette shook her head, making her tiger hat wobble. 'Not out here. The mist has ears. And it's not a who, it's a *what*.'

CHAPTER 11

Well, I tried to warn you. That's the trouble with being a book. You can use your very biggest print and nobody listens. Not even if you're a magic book of prophecy.

The Book

Ava slapped the mirror frame in frustration. Outside, the sun was still shining. Moonrise was hours away, and she was supposed to finish work in twenty minutes. How was she supposed to get back here at moonrise?

Mrs Footer opened the door and scowled to see Ava standing there. 'Whatever are you doing? You should have finished in here by now.'

'I'm sorry,' Ava said. 'Would you like me to stay late today?'

'No, I would not. I would like you to do your work on time.'

Ava supposed it had been too much to hope that Mrs Footer would agree. She picked up a vase to dust under it.

'Careful with that,' Mrs Footer snapped. 'You'll break it.'

Ava set it down a little harder than she meant to. 'Why do you dislike me so much?'

The words came out before she could stop them.

Mrs Footer's cheeks flushed scarlet. 'My son and I have gone out of our way to help you. We gave you a position here. I've tolerated all your mistakes. You should be repaying us by working hard, and instead you stand about dreaming.'

Ava knew she should be quiet, apologize and let this drop, but she couldn't. Nothing was right in this town and she was tired of it all.

'You're my aunt,' she said. 'I don't know what my father did to annoy you, but it has nothing to do with me.'

'Your father was an irresponsible man,' Mrs Footer said. 'He made a great many mistakes.'

Including her, she meant, Ava thought. She put her hand to the crescent mark on her cheek.

Mrs Footer looked away from her. 'I don't have time to stand talking. Mr Footer is appearing at the theatre tonight and I need to help him prepare. You can leave now.'

In the room off the kitchen, Ava collected her coat and bonnet in resentful silence. She imagined Howell waiting for her at moonrise, wondering where she was. And tomorrow was Sunday and she wouldn't be at work. She wouldn't get another chance to see him until Monday afternoon.

'Hurry up,' Mrs Footer snapped from the doorway.

Ava tied the ribbons on her bonnet. 'Coming.'

She dropped her gaze to the window. It was open at the bottom: a gap barely wide enough to put her fingers into.

Ava couldn't face going back home yet. Instead she walked to the high street and looked in the shop windows. The shopkeeper in the Wyse Emporium of Souvenirs saw her, and she waved at him cheekily.

Walking on, she spotted a small tourist office: *Maps, Books, Information. Gifts for Sale.*

Information: that was what she needed. Ava went inside.

The office was small and empty apart from a young woman sitting at a table. She looked up, frowned and went back to the book she was reading. Ava browsed the shelf of teapots and replica mirrors, then moved on to the guidebooks.

The magic mirrors control the fairy world, she read. *The process is perfectly safe. Fairy people are confined to the mirrors and may only come through into our world if ordered to do so by the conjuror. Such orders are rarely given. The six conjurors in Wyse are carefully monitored by our government minister, Lord Skinner, to ensure the magic mirrors are all operated safely*.

'Are you buying that?' the lady behind the table asked.

Ava shook her head and turned another page. Just a description of how conjurors supposedly kept their mirrors locked to stop magic leaking out.

'Do you know why magic mirrors stopped working?' Ava asked.

The lady put down the book she was reading. 'You're the Harcourt girl, aren't you?'

'Yes.' Ava saw how she looked away quickly from the mark on her cheek. 'Did you know my parents?' she asked.

'Not personally, no. I've heard people mention them.'

She'd heard the gossip, she meant, Ava thought. 'What about the mirrors? Why did they stop working? Do any of these books say?'

'They just stopped,' the lady said. 'No one knows why. There's no record of when the first one failed. I don't expect anyone thought it would be the start of all of them dying.' Her voice became almost mechanical. 'The first record we have is from seventeen ten, by which time fifty-three mirrors had ceased working.'

'And now we only have six left,' Ava said.

The lady rested her elbows on the table. 'Six is plenty. Some of the history books say it was quite chaotic before, with hundreds of working mirrors all over the country, and you never knew what you'd see when you looked into one. The system we have here is much better – everything properly controlled.'

Ava slid the book back on to the shelf. 'Do you know how long Lord Skinner has lived in Wyse?'

Did the lady's eyes glaze slightly? Ava wasn't sure. 'You should ask him,' she said. 'I'm sure he'll tell you. He's a fine gentleman.'

A fine gentleman. She was still no closer to finding out the truth. Ava went back to the main street and paused outside the theatre, reading the posters. Then, as she turned in the direction of home, she spotted a figure she recognized: small and round, wearing a cap and carrying a basket of bread.

'Charles!' Ava called.

He slowed when he heard her, and crossed the road to her. 'Hello, Ava. Did Mrs Footer send you out for something?'

'No, she sent me home early. Mr Footer's performing in the theatre tonight.'

Charles nodded. 'They take turns, all the conjurors.' He shifted his basket from arm to arm. 'You can walk with me if you like,' he offered. 'I've got two more deliveries left.'

Ava strolled along beside him, squinting in the sunlight. 'Do you know the other conjurors?'

'I deliver bread to them sometimes. There's Mr

Radcot – he lives across town. Then Mr Langhile and Mr Gaddesby, who are neighbours and work together. Mr Footer, of course. Then Mr Price, who is planning to retire and hand over to his son this year, and Mr Powell, who got married last year. His wife is expecting a baby.'

Six conjurors in the town and she had to get stuck with the Footers. Ava kicked a stone along as she walked. She had to get back into the Footers' house at moonrise.

Charles was still chattering about conjurors and magic.

'Charles,' Ava said, interrupting him. 'You know you said I could ask you for help if I needed it? Did you mean it?'

CHAPTER 12

Mirrors, like rules, are made to be broken. Well, both of them will cause a bit of a mess if you do, but it happens anyway. By the way, you might want to close your eyes in a page or two. Things are about to get unpleasant.

The Book

Lunette stopped outside a little shop with a red teapot sign over the door. Another sign read *Self-service: Please Come In*. It was well past teatime and the shop was empty. Lunette pulled a chair out at the nearest table and sat. A pot of tea, a china cup and a plate bearing a slice of strawberry cake appeared in front of her.

Howell remained in the doorway. The walk, although short, had cleared his mind and given him time to gather his courage.

'What is this about?' he asked. 'Mr Bones said you're an anti-humanist – is that true? Why shouldn't I trust him?'

'It's a little complicated.' Lunette set her bag on the floor. 'Would you like some tea?'

'You won't tell your hat to eat me?'

'This?' She pulled it off. 'It's only an illusion. I'm not an anti-humanist. I'm a hat-maker. I come from Unlyme on the west coast. It's a nice town, not much magic there now, but quiet and pleasant.'

That didn't explain anything. 'And Mr Bones?'

'Have you noticed that he never leaves Unwyse?' Lunette stirred sugar into her tea. 'I wonder why not. He's been around for ages too. At least a hundred years, probably much longer. You'd think he might have grown tired of Unwyse by now.'

'Maybe he's busy with Waxing Gibbous and the Mirror Station,' Howell said, wondering why it mattered where Mr Bones chose to live. He didn't trust Mr Bones, but it still felt slightly treasonous to be talking about him. 'Why do you care so much about him anyway?'

Lunette glanced up at him. 'I don't. But he wants something that is in my care.'

She bent and opened her bag.

Howell's feet carried him half a step forward, his insides a roiling mix of curiosity, worry and confusion, as Lunette reached into the bag, produced several hats and then a book.

That was all: an ordinary book, leather-bound and tattered at the edges, the cover plain apart from a pair of overlapping circles in the centre.

Mr Bones wanted a book? Everything inside Howell deflated.

'This isn't just any book,' Lunette said as if she'd read his thoughts. 'It's The Book. Capital T, capital B.' She opened it. The pages were all as blank as the cover. 'Book, this is Master Howell Fletcher.'

The Book's pages ruffled as if a breeze had passed over them, though Howell didn't feel anything. He walked closer, watching curiously as a dark spot squirmed to life right in the centre of the left-hand page, gradually spreading and forming words.

Lunette will speak with Master Fletcher, and they will leave quickly to the house with all the mirrors.

'What is this?' Howell breathed.

Letters blurred and rearranged themselves.

Made of paper, pages, spine, cover. I don't know what you think, but I'd say I'm a book. The Book, in fact. The Book of Unwyse Magic. I can tell you everything that is happening at this moment, and everything that will happen in every moment to come. Ask me a question.

Howell dragged his gaze off the page. 'Why are you called The Book of Unwyse Magic when you come from Unlyme?'

I don't come from Unlyme. I come from everywhere. The telephone will be invented in 1876, if 1876 ever happens, which is currently questionable.

Lunette sighed. 'The Book's been getting erratic lately, which is worrying. But when it makes sense you should pay attention.'

I am not an elephant, The Book wrote. *I mean erratic. Hello, Howell. You should sit down. Your future is looking interesting, by the way. Though, possibly, not very long.*

Howell sat: his legs seemed to want to. A teapot appeared and poured a stream of pale blue liquid into a cup. A tea party. None of this made any sense.

None of this makes sense to Howell, The Book echoed. *The electric oven won't be invented until 1890, probably later. The automobile will be invented around then as well. If there's anyone left to invent them.*

'What's an electric oven and an automobile?' Howell asked.

Lunette shook her head. 'It doesn't matter. The Book does this from time to time – making random predictions full of words I don't understand. It used to happen if I asked a question it couldn't answer, but it's been happening more often. I think it might be sickening from something.'

That was ridiculous: books didn't fall ill. But books didn't write things at you either. Howell shifted his weight in his chair. 'All right. You've got a talking book that tells the future, and Mr Bones wants it. What's this got to do with me?'

Lunette sipped her tea, frowning. 'I'm afraid I don't know. All I know is The Book told me I'd come to Unwyse and find you. It was a big risk, knowing that Mr Bones was hunting us, but, as I said, when The Book makes a prediction like that, you should pay attention and do as it says.'

The mirrors are dying – the future is in danger. Everything depends on you.

Howell swallowed a mouthful of salty tea, almost choking on it. 'What? But I've never even heard of The Book.'

Of course you haven't. I'm a secret. Don't travel on the Titanic *in 1912.*

'You're not a very useful book, you know,' Howell said.

Hey, you try foretelling the future and see how you get on. Oh dear.

The Book's pages turned blank, then two more words formed, squirming across the page in a hurry: *Leave. NOW*.

The words had such an urgency that Howell started to his feet. Outside, the light was fading. The moon would soon be rising.

Lunette stuffed The Book back into her bag. 'I'm coming with you.'

The House of Forgotten Mirrors was in darkness when they arrived. Howell opened the door a crack and peered inside. There was no one about.

'Come on in,' he whispered to Lunette, creeping inside. A faint glow of light started up from the ceiling, making the mirrors look more ghostly than ever. Across the room, he thought he saw something move and he jumped, then choked out a laugh. It was only a sheet, flapping in the draught from the door.

'Howell,' Lunette said quietly.

'It's safe.' Of course it was safe. Stupid book – and he was even stupider for believing it. Howell turned around, scanning the gallery. He'd been looking into mirror seventy-seven when he'd seen Ava. The mirror right over there.

The one that was uncovered with the sheet heaped on the floor beside it.

Something in Howell's chest jumped. It was fine, he told himself. He hadn't put the sheet back properly earlier and it had slid off, that was all.

Then he saw other sheets lying on the floor. A whole section of mirrors uncovered.

No, this wasn't fine. Master Tudur would never have left the mirrors like this, and Will was too lazy to bother messing them up. Howell took a step back towards the door. Where *was* Will?

It was then that he heard the noise.

It came softly at first, a rattling like fingernails skittering over glass. Then it grew louder and each click became more distinct. A hundred sharp claws tapping in a rhythm that made Howell think of . . .

Bones.

CHAPTER 13

Lunette and Howell will go to the House of Forgotten mirrors and . . . Oh dear. Can somebody else take over foreseeing the future here for a while? I'm going to see what's happening in the human world.

The Book

'Are you quite sure we won't get into trouble?' Charles asked. 'I want to be a policeman, remember. You're asking me to break the law.'

They stood a few houses down from the Footers', hiding behind a hedge. It was still light but the fairy lanterns were already beginning to glow dimly, making the air around them judder. Ava rubbed her eyes. She wasn't sure about this at all. 'It's not breaking the law,' she said. 'It's . . . investigating. All you have to do is knock on the door and keep Mrs Footer talking for a few minutes.'

'While you do what exactly?'

'It's a secret.' It was bad enough that she had to involve him in this. If he got into trouble, it would be her fault. 'It's to do with Freedom for Fair Folk,' she said. 'Please, just trust me.'

Charles shook his head, frowning. 'All right,' he agreed at last, balling his hands in his pockets. 'I'll ask her if she's seen my dog.'

'Do you have a dog?' Ava asked.

'No, but Mrs Footer doesn't know that.'

Ava sighed. It would do. 'Give me a minute, then knock on the door.'

She ran round the side of the house and made her way to the room at the back with the window that wouldn't close. She felt slightly ill, her hands so damp with sweat that her fingers stuck together. She wouldn't let herself think about what she was doing or she'd lose her nerve and run.

She squeezed her fingers into the gap under the window and heaved, edging the window open a little at a time, then she tucked her skirt up and climbed through.

Nobody screamed. Nobody came running, threatening to call the policeman. Ava let out a careful breath and tiptoed through the kitchen to the door.

What if Mrs Footer was entertaining friends in the parlour tonight? Ava froze, listening. She hadn't really thought past sneaking into the parlour, grabbing the enchantment off Howell and running before anyone saw her. It really was an awful idea, with any number of things that could go wrong.

Ava's hands shook. She dug her fingers into her skirt. Bad idea or not, she was here now, so she might as well try it.

The doorbell rang. Ava heard footsteps, and then voices.

'I haven't seen any dog,' Mrs Footer said.

'I think he may be trapped in your garden,' Charles replied. 'If you could just come while I look.' He said something else, too quiet for Ava to hear, and Mrs Footer sighed heavily.

'Oh, very well.' The front door closed.

Ava took a deep breath, then flung open the kitchen door and dashed along the hall to the parlour. It was empty. Her vision swam with relief as she closed the door behind her and faced the mirror.

'Come on, Howell,' she murmured. 'I'm here. Where are you?'

The sound of bones echoed through the House of Forgotten Mirrors. Howell tried to cry out but his voice had abandoned him. A skeleton stepped out of the shadows towards him, one hand outstretched. The dark bones glistened, the colour of bronze, and the empty eye sockets burned like candle flames.

'Howell Fletcher,' the lipless mouth whispered. 'You will come to Waxing Gibbous.'

The last word ended on a long hiss of air. Howell

felt a low moan rise in his chest. All the stories he'd heard about Mr Bones's skeletons were true.

The skeleton advanced on him, but he couldn't move – he couldn't even remember *how* to move. He stood frozen, not even able to blink and shut out the sight of the gaping eye sockets.

Then he felt Lunette's hand on his arm. She pushed him behind her, pushed her bag into his arms. 'Protect The Book,' she said, and tossed her hat on to the floor. It changed instantly, the tiger swishing its tail through the fallen sheets.

Howell gripped Lunette's bag, his arms sagging under the weight. This wasn't happening. It was a dream – a nightmare, more like. He'd wake up any minute and find himself safe in bed.

The tiger pounced. The skeleton grabbed it round the middle.

'Unfortunately, it is only an illusion,' Lunette murmured. 'Most people run away before they find that out.'

The skeleton thrust a bone hand right inside the tiger. It roared once, then vanished.

The bag slipped from Howell's grip.

The skeleton tore Lunette's hat in half and threw the pieces aside. 'The boy,' it whispered. Its voice was like cold mist, filling the whole gallery, smelling of sickness and decay.

Lunette picked up the hat-coat stand and swung it.

It was big and clumsy, but it drove the skeleton back a step.

'Don't worry,' she said, her voice coming in short gasps. 'I'm sure it's not as dangerous as it looks.'

They were going to die, Howell thought. Master Tudur would find his body here, or Will would, if Will was still alive – maybe the skeleton had killed him already. The thought wasn't any comfort.

Lunette swung the coat-stand again. The skeleton caught it and wrenched it out of her grip. The fear that had held Howell immobile snapped. His ears filled up with a roaring sound.

'Let her go!' he shouted. He snatched up a dust sheet and lashed out with it wildly, hitting a mirror instead.

The glass turned to mist and then cleared. Howell saw Ava's startled face looking out at him.

Relief coursed through him. 'Ava!' he cried. 'Invite us through!'

Ava stared at him stupidly. 'What?'

She was arguing? When he was about to be murdered. 'Do it!'

The skeleton threw the coat-stand aside and grabbed Howell instead. Howell screamed and struck out but the bone hands held him fast.

'Howell!' Lunette shouted. She picked up the fallen coat-stand and hit the skeleton with it. The skeleton staggered sideways, its grip loosening enough for

Howell to struggle free. He landed hard on his hands and knees, facing the mirror where Ava watched.

Finally she seemed to understand something was wrong. She struck the glass from her side. 'Come through. I *order* you to come through.'

Howell scrambled back to his feet, looked around to find Lunette and saw her right behind him.

'Go!' she shouted. She shoved him at the glass. The mirror turned to mist. Howell yelled. Bone hands groped for him, but he was already falling out of reach, his hands twisting into Lunette's dress as the Unworld disappeared around him.

CHAPTER 14

Is it safe to come out yet? Don't blame me for hiding. You people should take better care of books. Don't crease our spines, don't bend our corners and, above all, keep us away from angry skeletons.

The Book

Ava stumbled back, shielding her eyes as the mirror turned bright with mist. A second later, Howell burst out backwards into her, and, before Ava could recover, a lady with pink hair fell through as well, and landed on top of them both.

The front door banged. Ava squirmed free and stood up. 'What in the world . . .'

A hand appeared in the mirror – a hand made entirely of bone.

'Don't let it through!' Howell shouted.

Ava didn't think. She grabbed the poker from the fireside and hit the mirror as hard as she could. She couldn't see the glass for mist, but she heard it break – a crack louder than lightning, as if something far more than ordinary glass had shattered. Bone fingers wrapped round her wrist. She screamed and hit the mirror again. The skeletal grip loosened, the hand turning grey as it dissolved back into the mist. As the first shards of glass began to fall on to the carpet, it vanished.

Ava stood panting, still clutching the poker.

'You broke the mirror,' Howell said. His eyes were round, his face pale beneath the green spikes of his hair.

'I know. Are you all right?'

He nodded and put a hand in his pocket. 'I . . .'

The door flew open.

Mrs Footer shrieked. 'My mirror!'

Ava groaned. 'Mrs Footer, please let me explain.'

'Explain what?' Then she saw Howell, and the lady with pink hair, and she screamed again. 'You invited strangers into my house!'

Howell tried to sidle towards the door.

Mrs Footer caught him by the ear. 'You stay where you are. I'm calling the police.'

'Let me go!' Howell flailed at her, his closed fist striking her in the middle. The room filled with silver light and the musky scent of lavender.

Ava sneezed.

The light faded back to normal.

Mrs Footer was gone. In her place . . .

Ava rubbed her eyes, blinked and rubbed her eyes

again, unable to believe what she was seeing . . .

Where Mrs Footer had been standing, a small black and white dog danced about on the carpet, yapping frantically.

If that was an illusion, it was the best one Ava had ever seen.

The Unworld lady cleared her throat delicately. 'Um, hello, my name is Lunette. I'm very pleased to meet you. The weather is pleasant for the time of year.'

Ava tore her gaze away from Mrs Footer. 'What?'

Lunette smiled and shrugged. 'I thought humans always talked about the weather.'

Ava shook her head, trying to focus. 'No. Not always. Sometimes we talk about things like . . . what on earth are you doing here and why is Mrs Footer a *dog*?' Her voice shook. She put a hand out to the dog, expecting to feel Mrs Footer's bonnet, but her fingers touched a pair of floppy ears, and short, scratchy hair.

Howell backed away. 'That's a dog? I've heard stories about your dogs – they eat people.'

'What? No they don't.' Ava hoped this was a dream because none of it was making any sense. What was Matthew going to say when he found out? She sucked in a breath. 'Turn Mrs Footer back at once.'

'I can't,' Howell said. 'That was your enchantment, to reveal the truth about someone.

'I got it from my aunt,' Lunette said, nibbling her bottom lip worriedly. 'I'm sure it'll wear off eventually.'

Ava crouched down to study the little dog. She couldn't see any aura from the enchantment, no sign that Mrs Footer was anything other than a common terrier. If the cheap enchantments in the souvenir shops could last a few weeks, how long would this one last?

And then, as if the evening wasn't bad enough, Ava heard Charles in the hall.

'Ava? I heard shouting. Is everything all right?'

'Don't come in,' Ava shouted, just as Charles appeared in the doorway. His mouth fell open.

'Fair Folk,' he said. 'Wow.'

For several seconds no one moved. Ava spoke first. 'Um, this is my friend, Charles Brunel,' she said. 'Charles, these are Howell and Lunette from Unwyse.'

'Actually, I'm from Unlyme,' Lunette murmured. She held out her hand to Charles. 'Pleased to meet you.'

'Likewise.' He shook hands, a huge grin on his face. 'My mother is the secretary for the League for Freedom for Fair Folk.' His gaze fell on the dog. 'Ava, if you'd said you had a dog, I needn't have lied to Mrs Footer.'

'That *is* Mrs Footer,' Ava said. 'Howell enchanted her by mistake.'

Charles's eyes popped. 'Really? It's a good enchantment. Isn't she going to be cross when she turns back?'

'I expect so.' Ava pulled off her bonnet and ran a hand through her hair. She needed Charles to be serious and he was treating this like a game. 'What are we going to do?'

'Well, Mum did want to invite you to dinner,' Charles said. 'And my house is closer. Why don't we go there?' He picked a piece of glass off the carpet and breathed on it, turning its surface to mist, then placed it carefully back down.

'I suppose so,' Ava said uncertainly. Going to the Brunels' house would at least delay the moment when she had to face Matthew. 'Thank you.'

Lunette opened her bag and pulled out a wide-brimmed yellow-silk creation that really shouldn't have fitted in there. 'My camouflage hat,' she said, putting it on.

Ava couldn't imagine something more likely to draw attention – except maybe here in Wyse, where every holidaymaker competed to stand out.

Charles sniffed. 'Can anyone smell apples, by the way?'

Ava could smell it too. She looked back at the broken mirror. A thin strand of white mist was curling out. As she watched, it sank into the carpet and, where it touched, the carpet turned the same yellow as Lunette's hat.

'What's that?' Ava asked, but by the time Charles looked, it had already gone back to normal.

CHAPTER 15

One of the problems is that human people don't really believe in magic any more. It is a curiosity, entertaining and with just enough danger to make it interesting, like a fast carriage ride through the park.

Most fairy magic is not like that, but, by the time you humans learn that, it is usually too late.

Those bits of broken mirror, for example. Some of them are turning misty. But you probably don't care.

The Book

No mist. That was Howell's first thought. The evening air was warm and clear, and in the naked moonlight all the edges of the houses stood out in sharp focus. The air didn't smell of anything, either; instead, scent came in gusts from houses as they passed: food cooking, over-sweet perfume from gardens. Every time a new smell hit him, it made him want to sneeze.

Charles and Ava hurried on and didn't seem to notice the lack of mist. Maybe the human world was supposed to be like this.

'How long have you two been communicating?' Charles asked.

Ava glanced back at Howell. 'Since about a week ago.'

'And you didn't say?'

'What was I supposed to say – "Hello, Charles, isn't the weather nice and, by the way, I've been talking to one of the Fair Folk through a mirror that shouldn't work"?' She smiled, but Howell saw the worry in her eyes.

He hadn't been the only one who'd struggled to keep this secret, he thought. Well, the secret was out now.

'Don't ask me what happened,' he said. 'All I know is I was cleaning the mirror when Ava appeared in it.'

Oddly, Charles appeared pleased. 'It's a mystery, then. Good.'

It might be good for Charles. He wasn't the one stuck in the wrong world.

A carriage rattled by, covered all over in poor-quality enchantments. The two horses seemed impossibly large in the narrow street. Howell shrank back from them.

'Don't you have horses in Unwyse?' Charles asked.

'Of course we do. But they're all wild.' Unworld horses had manes and tails of pure flame. If you were silly enough to try harnessing them to a carriage, they'd burn it to a cinder. Howell looked down at Mrs Footer, running along beside Ava. He wasn't sure he liked this bright, too-warm world where nothing was as it should be.

They turned a corner on to a road where a large, stone building with a cross above the door stood opposite a row of houses. Charles knocked on the second door.

How did humans greet each other? Howell wondered. Before he could ask, the door opened. A large, dark-haired lady stood there, wiping her hands on an apron.

'Charles, where have you . . .' she began and broke off. 'Oh, my. You'd better all come inside.'

Until today, the only thing Howell had known for certain about humans was they had no magic of their own and so they kept demanding enchantments to make their lives easier. But Charles's mother was a whirlwind of activity. First she sent Charles's sisters to fetch Ava's brother, and then she made Howell and Lunette sit by the fire, asked every minute if they were all right and brought them cups of something she said was tea, though it was pale brown instead of blue and tasted milky and sweet. Howell considered asking if she had any salt he could add, but everyone else seemed to be drinking it happily so he sipped his slowly, hoping he'd get used to it.

'Shall I put your bag somewhere safe?' Mr Brunel offered.

Lunette shook her head. She'd taken off her hat and her hair drooped in pink curls. 'Thank you, but it's safest here with me.'

Howell was wondering where Ava had gone when she came into the room. 'Mrs Footer is in the kitchen. Thank you for letting us stay here.'

'Don't mention it,' said Mrs Brunel. 'More tea, anyone?'

Howell shook his head. He wished everyone would stop smiling at him; it was unnerving.

'This is so amazing,' Charles said.

Howell didn't think any of it was amazing. It was unreal, terrifying. He was in Wyse; he'd been attacked by a skeleton. He hunched lower in his chair. The skeleton had to be Mr Bones's doing – but why would Mr Bones send a skeleton after him? He could have found Howell in the House of Forgotten Mirrors any time.

Because of Lunette and The Book, of course, he thought. Mr Bones wanted The Book and he must have found out Lunette was looking for Howell. That was why he'd kept asking if Howell had seen her – he was hoping Howell would lead him to her.

Howell shuddered. If Ava hadn't called him through the mirror, he and Lunette would be prisoners by now.

Then the door opened and Charles's two sisters

came in, accompanied by a young man with frizzy brown hair and wide, worried grey eyes.

Ava jumped up. 'Matthew. I can explain.'

'I certainly hope so,' Matthew said. 'Your friends were babbling about fairy visitors and people turning into dogs, and . . .' He stopped, his mouth still open. A few strangled sounds came out of it while his face turned the same strawberry pink as Lunette's hair.

Lunette stood. 'Please don't be angry at Ava. She saved our lives. If she hadn't invited us through the mirror, Howell and I would have been dragged into captivity by a skeleton.'

Matthew's cheeks tried out several shades from strawberry to plum and back. 'It's no bother,' he said weakly. He sat down heavily, clutching his hat on his lap. 'A skeleton? Will someone please tell me what is going on?'

Howell let Ava do most of the talking: she seemed to want to. He sat, his empty teacup on his knee, trying to pretend he hadn't noticed how Charles's sisters kept staring at his hair. In the end, Mrs Brunel shooed them both out and shut the door firmly.

'They won't tell anyone,' she whispered to Howell. 'None of us will.'

He ought to have felt grateful, but he didn't have room for anything besides bewilderment.

'. . . And then Mrs Footer turned into a dog,' Ava said. 'A real dog.'

Matthew almost dropped his cup. 'That's impossible. Fairy magic is only illusion.'

'You'd be surprised what fairy magic can do,' Lunette said. 'Magic brings things to life, it transforms and destroys. It all depends on what kind of magic is used and who uses it.'

Once again, Howell saw a pair of skeleton hands reaching for him, and his teacup rattled in its saucer.

'Where is Mrs Footer now?' Matthew asked.

Ava picked at her skirt. 'The kitchen. Mrs Brunel found her a bone.'

Matthew smiled at this, and quickly covered it up with a stern frown.

'It was an accident,' Ava said. 'The enchantment was meant for Lord Skinner.'

'You wanted to turn Lord Skinner into a dog?'

'No, I wanted to find out the truth about him.'

'The enchantment brings out a person's true nature,' Lunette explained with an apologetic shrug. 'It appears your Mrs Footer was doggish. The enchantment will wear off in time.'

Matthew heaved a sigh and slumped back in his chair. Howell couldn't help feeling sorry for him. He looked nice – nice, and confused, and slightly battered by all this information.

'I suppose we shall just have to tell Mr Footer

everything,' Matthew said. 'He might be able to take the enchantment off. And he can send Lunette and Howell back to the Unworld.' He cast a glance at Lunette and blushed again. 'I assume he can. I don't really know how these things work.'

Howell felt a prickle of alarm across his back. They couldn't go back, though, not now. 'Every working mirror in Wyse is paired to one in Unwyse,' he said, 'and all the Unwyse mirrors are in the Mirror Station. If we go back, that's where we'll end up, and Mr Bones will be waiting for us.'

'Mr Bones?' asked Matthew.

Howell really didn't want to talk about it. 'Mr Bones rules Unwyse. People say he saved the last mirrors when all the others were dying. And he can create skeletons out of mist to hunt down people who disobey him.'

'People like you, you mean,' Matthew said. 'What did you do to make him come after you?'

Howell hunched his shoulders and said nothing.

'It's not what we did,' Lunette said. 'It's what we're guarding.'

Howell caught his breath. They'd only just met these humans and, though he liked them, he didn't know how much they could trust them.

Lunette, however, seemed entirely unconcerned as she reached into her bag and laid The Book on her lap. 'This is The Book,' she said, opening it. 'It foretells the future – in a manner of speaking. It's not being very helpful at the moment.'

An ink blot moved.

I heard that.

Mr and Mrs Brunel jumped up and Charles fell off his chair altogether.

Hey, look at that, The Book wrote. *My magic still works this side of the mirror. Hello, everyone. I am The Book of Unwyse Magic. I knew I was going to meet you, but it's still exciting.*

'Hello, Book,' Ava said uncertainly. Matthew leaned forward, catching her hand before she could touch the yellowed pages.

You're here, The Book wrote. *Good. Time is a precious thing so it's always useful if we can save some of it.*

'What's it talking about?' Ava asked.

Letters scrambled and reformed.

The mirrors are dying. The covenant is under threat and the future of the two worlds with it. You can forget about going back to Unwyse for now. Master Howell Fletcher, Miss Ava Harcourt, from this moment you two are my new guardians.

CHAPTER 16

The Book's guardian changes every seven years. Their task is to protect me and not drop me in the bath, for example. It's usually quite an easy job. It's going to be different this time, though. Two guardians. Twice the trouble.

The Book

Ava had been practising deep breaths, trying to keep calm despite the growing panic on Matthew's face, but then the scrawling letters spelled out her own name.

She swallowed a yelp of surprise and drew her hand out of Matthew's grip. 'There must be a mistake,' she said. 'How can I be a guardian of a fairy book?'

Lunette's lips drew tight. 'You can't be. The Book is getting confused again. It only had one guardian at a time. I think it must mean that Howell is going to be its new guardian after me.'

You might not have noticed, The Book wrote stiffly, *but I am a book. I know how to use words. If I say Howell and Ava are my guardians, then that is what they are. Both of them, from this moment on. They are connected by magic.*

The words vanished, letter by letter.

Ava's skin was like ice, her heart thudding inside her chest.

'Connected how?' Howell asked. His face had turned greenish to match his hair. 'We never even met until a few days ago. How can we be connected?'

I don't do the past. Did you know that London is currently the largest city in the world and it's going to get bigger? People in London don't need magic because they have technology.

'It's babbling again,' Lunette said, frowning. 'Book, you could have told me sooner that Howell was going to be your new guardian.'

The Book flapped its pages. *That bit of the future has only just decided to happen. This isn't easy, you know. Maybe you shouldn't have dropped me in the bath if you wanted me to work properly. Ava and Howell are connected. This is why they can reopen closed mirrors: their connection brings old connections back to life.*

Ava read the words over and over until they faded but they still made no sense.

She'd always known that something wasn't quite right about her – the mark on her face, the whispers about fairy magic, the way everyone looked at her strangely. Matthew had always denied it, but he must have wondered. The knowledge made her feel completely alone. She rubbed the mark on her cheek.

'I've got one of those, too,' Howell said, rolling back his sleeve to show her.

His mark was a perfect circle, the right size to fit inside hers.

'Coincidence,' Matthew said.

Charles looked up from his notebook. 'Some would say a coincidence is just another word for a clue.'

'And some would say fairy magic is not to be trusted,' Matthew said. 'That includes a magic book.'

The Book's pages fluttered again. *Matthew Harcourt doesn't want to believe this. He is afraid. The mirrors are dying. Ava and Howell can save them . . . or not. Whatever happens, everything must change.*

'What exactly is that supposed to mean?' Matthew asked.

Ava met Howell's gaze. He shrugged. Mr and Mrs Brunel were both frowning and Ava wondered if they regretted getting involved in this.

'I can guess part of it,' Charles said. 'Ava and Howell met through a magic mirror that was long dead. What if they can do it again? They might be able to bring all the mirrors back to life.'

The past had been chaotic, the lady in the tourist office had said. Ava felt a shiver go through her – *hundreds of working mirrors*. She thought of all the mirrors hanging in Waning Crescent, of Lord Skinner watching her hungrily, and she wanted to run, and keep running until she'd left Wyse far behind.

'What should we do?' she asked.

'Howell and Lunette can stay here,' Charles said. 'Can't they, Mum?'

Ava shook her head. 'They should stay with Matthew and me.' She looked at Matthew, expecting him to agree, but he frowned and avoided her gaze.

'No,' he said. 'I'm sorry, but no. Ava, you're my sister and I'm responsible for you. Miss Lunette, I'm afraid you'll need to find a new guardian for your book.' He stood up. 'Ava, please fetch your coat, and Mrs Footer.'

'Matthew!' Ava cried.

'I mean it.' He still wouldn't look at her. 'We'll tell Mr Footer everything and he can send Howell and Lunette back to the Unworld.' His cheeks turned pink as he turned to Lunette. 'I really am very sorry.'

'I can't believe you just did that,' Ava burst out as soon as they were outside.

Mrs Footer stopped to wee against a hedge, then she shook herself and nipped Ava's ankle, as if blaming her entirely for the humiliation.

'The Book could be wrong,' Matthew said. 'Fairy magic is unreliable. You shouldn't have been messing around with mirrors in the first place.'

'So it's all my fault now.'

'Yes, it is, actually.'

He had a point. Ava paused in the road, arms folded. 'What happens if we send Howell and Lunette home and Mr Bones catches them? Or do you not care, as long as nothing happens to us?'

Mrs Footer growled at her. Matthew sighed. 'Of course I care, but I promised Father I'd look after you. These last few months have been hard enough already.'

And harder still because of her, he meant.

'We'll talk to Mr Footer,' Matthew said. 'And if he can't help, I'll ask Lord Skinner for advice. He's—'

'A fine gentleman?' Ava said sarcastically. She tugged Mrs Footer along ahead of Matthew so she wouldn't have to speak to him.

She strode ahead all the way to the Footers' house, then she slowed, her heart sinking. Mr Footer was home and he wasn't alone. A small group of neighbours clustered around him – Ava recognized some of them. Mr Footer stood in the middle, wearing a silver suit and a cloak that kept changing colour. His moustache was waxed into ridiculous curls.

'Mr Footer,' Matthew said.

Everyone turned to stare at them.

'We need to talk to you,' Ava said. 'It's very important.'

'More important than my mother disappearing?

This is hardly the time for a family visit, Mr Harcourt.'

Mrs Footer wriggled in Ava's arms and almost slipped free.

'Take that dog away,' Mr Footer said. 'I can't stand dogs.'

'Five minutes,' Matthew said. 'Please.'

The conjuror looked around at the surrounding neighbours. He really didn't know what to do without his mother barking instructions at him, Ava thought. She glanced at Matthew, his pale, determined face, and a knot formed in her chest. He'd tell Mr Footer everything, Howell and Lunette would go back to Unwyse, and all this – whatever this really was – would be over before it had started.

'Someone send for Constable Blackson,' Mr Footer said. 'The police should be informed. Five minutes, Mr Harcourt.'

But before they could take a step towards the house, Ava heard the rattle of carriage wheels. She turned to look and her insides froze. Lord Skinner was here.

He rode in a dark carriage that was perfectly plain, not a single enchantment clinging to it.

Mr Footer brushed past Ava as if she wasn't there. 'Lord Skinner, thank goodness you're here. I came home this evening to find the front door open, glass all over the floor and my mother vanished without trace. I know she had no plans to go out tonight.'

Lord Skinner stepped out of his carriage and took

off his hat. Ava could see his scalp through his hair, the skin drooping like folds of damp paper. She let out a slow breath. Lord Skinner would sort everything out. He was a . . .

No! He was *not* a fine gentleman. He'd tricked everyone into thinking he was, but it wasn't true. Ava shook her head and clenched her nails into her palms, concentrating on the sharp spots of pain.

And, just like that, she knew that everything about Lord Skinner was fake. He still looked the same, but something had changed, as if an illusion had finally been stripped away. He wanted to be liked, he wanted to be in charge, he wanted . . .

Something brushed against her skirt and she looked down to see a yellow frog hopping past. Lord Skinner bent to pick it up and an odd smile crossed his face. As if something he'd been waiting for had finally happened. He released the frog and straightened.

'Miss Harcourt, what do you know about the broken mirror?' he asked.

Not *if* she knew anything, but *what*. He already knew she'd had something to do with it. Ava pinched Matthew. 'Nothing. Mrs Footer sent me home early today. I stopped by the tourist office – you can check with the lady who works there.'

'I'll do that.' He looked away and Ava felt as if a shadow had passed away from her.

'Mr Footer,' he said, 'I need to talk to you. We may

be facing an attack from the Unworld.'

The group of neighbours fell silent, then all started talking at once.

Mr Footer's mouth fell open. 'Impossible. The Unworld isn't real.'

'It's more real than you think, I'm afraid,' Lord Skinner said. 'Something has come into our world – something dangerous, something *other*. We must find it before it can do any more harm.'

He was talking about Howell and Lunette, Ava thought, but he couldn't possibly know about them. He was making this up to frighten people and it was working. Mr Footer turned pale. The neighbours huddled closer to him, watching the bushes as if they expected Unworld creatures to leap out.

'Miss Harcourt,' Lord Skinner said, 'I see you have a pet.'

Ava froze. Mrs Footer growled and snapped. 'Sorry,' Ava said insincerely. 'She doesn't like strangers.'

'She's a sensible dog.' His gaze bored into Ava. 'What's her name?'

'Spot,' Ava said.

'Patch,' Matthew said.

Ava's face grew hot. 'Spatch. We found her living in our garden. We couldn't agree on a name.'

'I see.' He studied the little dog hard. 'She seems to be an ordinary dog.'

'What else would she be?' Ava asked innocently.

The scent of damp leaves surrounded her. All along the street, the fairy lights flickered and turned misty.

'You should go home,' Lord Skinner said. 'Be on your guard for fairy creatures. Mr Footer, if you please.'

Matthew took a step after them, but Ava caught his coat-tails to stop him. Lord Skinner and Mr Footer went into the house together. The neighbours left, brushing past Ava and Matthew without a word.

'Why did you stop me?' Matthew asked after the last one had gone. 'We should have told him.'

'No, we really shouldn't. You saw him lie to everyone. Lord Skinner is not a fine gentleman. He knows far more about fairy magic than he pretends. Please, think. He invites us to dinner all the time, he keeps asking me about magic mirrors. That isn't normal.'

The Footers' front door opened again abruptly.

'Mr Harcourt,' Lord Skinner called.

Ava's breath juddered to a stop.

Lord Skinner gave her a searching stare. 'Work must continue,' he said. 'Eight thirty, Monday morning. Unless there's anything else?'

Ava held her breath.

Matthew clenched his fists, then slowly he shook his head. 'No, there's nothing else. Goodnight, Lord Skinner. Come along, Ava.'

He strode away so fast Ava had to run to catch up

with him. 'You believe me! You do, don't you?'

'Maybe. I'm not sure.' He slowed. 'Right now, I don't know what to think,' he said. 'But maybe we should keep this quiet until we know what's going on. Lunette and Howell can stay with us tonight, and tomorrow . . . Well, we'll see what we can find out.' He gave a strained smile. 'We must maintain our sense of adventure, after all.'

Ava hugged him. 'Thank you.'

It was getting cold all of a sudden and the lamps on the main street flickered on and off, making everything look strange and unworldly. Mrs Footer whined softly.

Ava shivered. She was the guardian of a magic book. She was connected to a fairy boy – and Lord Skinner was watching her.

CHAPTER 17

If you're worried about fairy monsters bursting through your mirrors, by the way, don't be. It almost definitely won't happen. It probably won't happen. Well, it might happen, but worrying about it won't change anything.

The Book

Howell woke the next morning with strange warm sunlight crawling across his face. He lay for a moment, wondering where he was and why he was on the floor, then he remembered and scrambled free of his blanket. The inside of his head was a chaos of talking skeletons, breaking glass and sarcastic books. He rubbed his hands over his face and smelled lavender on his palms.

He realized someone had spoken and he turned round to see Ava standing in the doorway. Instead of her dark grey dress she wore a light brown one and her hair was pinned up, making her look older than yesterday – or maybe a sleepless night had done that to her.

Neither she nor Matthew had said very much when they'd returned from the Footers' home last night, only that Howell and Lunette would be staying the night after all, but as they'd brought Mrs Footer back in dog form he guessed the conversation with Mr Footer hadn't gone well.

'It's Sunday,' Ava said. 'We have to go to church or people will wonder why we're not there. Matthew thinks it'd be best if you and Lunette stay here. Are you hungry? We have sausages and bacon and eggs. Or there's cheese and bread. What do you eat?'

Howell's stomach growled. He hadn't even seen any food since yesterday afternoon, and he'd barely tasted that.

'Food,' he said. 'I eat food. Anything is fine.'

They continued looking at each other. Ava in the mirror had seemed very different to the girl who stood in the doorway. Back then, she'd appeared quite sure of herself. Now, she looked nervous and tugged at her skirt as if her clothes didn't fit her properly.

Howell combed his fingers through his hair. He wished he knew what was happening back in Unwyse. Mr Bones would know he'd escaped by now. And what about Master Tudur and Will?

'So, we're the guardians of The Book. Both of us together.'

Ava nodded. 'The Book said we were connected, but how? We're from separate worlds.'

But the worlds were connected, Howell thought, by the mirrors and the covenant. 'The Book said the covenant was under threat. And Mr Bones asked me about it too. He seemed to think it could be changed.'

'What *is* the covenant?' Ava asked. 'Charles said there's an old story that the Fair Folk took magic from this world to make the Unworld and gave us the mirrors in exchange. Is that true?'

'More or less. Any magical goods or services requested through the mirrors have to be supplied. And if the covenant is broken, all magic will leave the Unworld. Which probably means the Unworld will cease to exist, but no one really knows.'

'I'm sorry,' Ava said.

'Don't be. The covenant was written long ago. It's always been the same.' He dropped his gaze. His clothes were crumpled from sleeping in them and he guessed he could probably do with a wash. His stomach growled.

'Breakfast,' Ava said.

They found Lunette and Matthew sitting either side of the kitchen table with a pile of hats between them.

'This is my camouflage hat,' Lunette was saying, holding up a bonnet in mottled greens and browns. She reached for a plain white creation. 'And here's my disguise hat. This one is my hat for cold weather, and my hat for wet weather, and my climbing hat and running hat. I have one of everything.'

'And they all fit in that bag,' Matthew said.

'Of course they do – it's a hat bag. I did also have an attack hat, but the skeleton broke that one. If I was in the Unworld, it would have grown back already, but hats need magic to grow.'

'She grows hats?' Ava whispered.

Howell shrugged. 'It's an Unworld thing. There are different kinds of magic. *You* only see common enchantments. They're created by pulling magic out of the air, and because air is weak, the enchantments are weak. But some enchantments are stronger – the one that changed Mrs Footer, for example.'

He glanced over at the dog curled up by the stove. Mrs Footer raised her head and growled softly, and Howell edged back behind Ava. Dogs might be harmless in this world, but he wasn't taking any chances.

'Most people, though,' he said, 'don't just use magic, they *are* magical.'

'Especially in Unwyse,' Lunette said. 'There's more magic there than anywhere else in the Unworld. The mirrors attract it. When you grow up with that much magic, it changes you. My speciality is hats, but I've got an aunt, Madame Brille, who makes enchantments and can see anything.'

'I think hats is a charming speciality,' Matthew said. 'It suits you.'

Lunette blushed. 'Thank you.'

'What's your speciality?' Ava asked Howell.

He shrugged uncomfortably. 'I don't have one. I'm completely ordinary. That's why I was sent to work in the House of Forgotten Mirrors, because you don't need any magic to polish glass.'

Ava tossed her head and sniffed. 'Nobody is completely ordinary. The Book chose you – that's got to mean something.'

Maybe it did mean something, but Howell didn't know what. He didn't feel any more magical because The Book had chosen him.

Lunette moved hats aside and reached for her bag. 'Would you like a Sunday hat, Howell? Humans dress up on Sundays – it's the tradition.'

Howell tried to tug his shirt straight. *If humans cared less about what things looked like and more about how things actually were, their world might be very different*, he thought.

He walked to the window and looked out. The morning was bright and there was even a thread of mist twisting across the garden, shimmering where the sunlight glanced off it. He stretched his arms, easing the stiffness out of his shoulders. He was in the human world – this ought to be an adventure.

He turned back to the table. Ava had promised breakfast, but she was opening The Book instead.

Where were you? You're supposed to be my guardians. All sorts of bad things are or will be happening, and my guardians only care about hats and breakfast.

'We're here now, aren't we?' Howell said. 'If Ava and I are your guardians, you ought to explain what's going on. Why is Mr Bones after you?'

'And what about Lord Skinner?' Ava added. 'Why did Lord Skinner invite Matthew and me back to Wyse?'

I told you, I don't do the past.

Howell rubbed a hand through his hair. 'All right. What if we investigate? Suppose we do it very carefully and find out exactly what's going on here. What will we learn?'

The Book was still for a moment. *The first Sherlock Holmes story will be written in 1887. Mr Bones knows where you are. You'll have to wait until 1897 for* Dracula, *but you'll have* Jekyll and Hyde *by 1886. What is written must come to pass.*

'I think it means it can't tell you,' Lunette said. 'Either that or it's going wrong again.'

I am quite well, thank you. You're not listening. It's this world that is going wrong. It's forgotten what it's like to have magic.

The words faded.

Howell sat and stared at the blank page. He didn't know what 'Jekyll and Hyde' was, but *What is written must come to pass* – those were the last words of the covenant.

Lunette patted him on the shoulder. 'We'll be safe here while we work it out. As I said, I've never known Mr Bones to leave Unwyse. He won't find us here.'

Mr Bones might be the least of their worries right now, Howell thought. He leaned his elbows on the table either side of The Book.

'Book,' he said again, 'why does Mr Bones want you?'

The Book didn't respond.

'Breakfast,' Matthew said, 'and then church. We'll discuss all this later.'

They'd have to discuss loads of things later, Howell thought, such as what in the Unworld were they going to do?

The church pews were crowded that morning, almost the whole town whispering about the Unworld. Mr Footer was absent, though, Ava noticed – and so was Lord Skinner. His pew stood noticeably empty at the front.

Charles waved at Ava as the Brunels came in, and mouthed something at her, which she couldn't make out. She waved back, wishing the service was over already so they could talk. They needed a plan.

She fidgeted through the sermon, barely hearing a word.

Where was Lord Skinner this morning? In hiding? That didn't seem likely. The man was a complete mystery, Ava thought. He lived alone, he'd never mentioned any family or anything about his life.

Actually, there was something. Ava sat up straighter. That very first evening she and Matthew had dined with him, he'd told them Waning Crescent had once been a museum to magic and when he'd 'moved back' he'd decided to keep all the mirrors as a reminder. He'd moved back – which meant he'd lived here once before. Maybe his whole family had come from Wyse originally.

The chords of the final hymn made Ava jump. She scrambled for her hymn book, almost dropping it in her haste. That was odd – the book was bright green. Hadn't it been brown a moment ago?

Then a bird burst out of the flower arrangement at the front of the church, swooped over the heads of the startled congregation and flew out of the door.

'Must have been sleeping right through my sermon,' Reverend Stowe joked, but his laughter sounded forced and he edged away from the flowers as if they'd become poisonous.

The moment the service finished, people streamed out of the church, pushing one another in their haste.

'Everyone's talking about Fair Folk,' Charles said, making his way across to join Ava. 'They all think we're under attack.'

'That's silly. Nothing's happened yet.'

'It doesn't take much to get people gossiping,' Charles said.

Reverend Stowe shook hands with them at the door. 'It's nice to see you're making friends.' He leaned closer and added in a whisper, 'I hear there was some excitement last night.'

'Nothing to worry about,' Matthew said, his hand on Ava's back.

She dug her heels into the mat.

'Actually, Reverend Stowe,' she said, 'you might be able to help. Somebody said Lord Skinner came from Wyse originally and moved away before coming back here. Is that true?'

Reverend Stowe gave her a confused smile. 'I believe it is. I couldn't say for sure, however. As I said, I've only been in Wyse a few years myself.'

Fortunately, they didn't have to rely on Reverend Stowe's memory. 'Does the church have family records?' Ava asked. She glanced at Charles and saw him nodding. 'Maybe we could take a look this afternoon.'

CHAPTER 18

British people always talk about the weather. They always have and they always will. They're never satisfied, either. It's either too hot or too cold, too wet or too dry or too windy. I have no idea why they do this. Maybe it distracts them from more important considerations, such as the fact that the world is quite possibly doomed.

The Book

The weather felt wrong that afternoon, more autumn than summer. Little strands of mist curled around the house and drifted in through the door when Ava opened it to let Charles in, and the air outside smelled of apples, as if someone was baking a pie.

Howell wore a flat cap similar to Charles's except he kept his low over his ears, and Lunette had chosen a giant, floppy creation covered in spiky, bright green net.

'I'd still prefer it if you and Howell stayed in the house,' Matthew said.

Lunette tucked her hand through his arm. 'Nonsense. We'll be far safer with you, and we want to help.'

Matthew's cheeks turned pink. 'Um. Well, yes, I suppose . . .'

Ava grinned to see him flustered.

'If anyone asks,' Matthew said, 'and they won't because we're all British here and far too polite, you're my cousins, visiting from Cambridgeshire. If they want to know what it's like there, say that it rains a lot.'

The sound of organ music greeted them as they made their way between gravestones to the church doors.

'Reverend Stowe practises when no one is around,' Charles said, wincing at a thunderous series of wrong notes. He banged on the door, then opened it without waiting for an answer.

The organ stopped, mercifully, and Reverend Stowe came hurrying to meet them a moment later.

'Hello,' Matthew said. 'I've brought my cousins – from Cambridge.'

The reverend paused when he saw Lunette and Howell. Lunette raised her hand in a wave.

'Cambridge, yes of course,' Reverend Stowe said, rubbing his forehead. 'We're all cousins in one sense. Do come on in. I'm sorry not to have seen you at the service this morning. I see you've brought your dog too.'

Ava picked Mrs Footer up. 'I'm sorry. We couldn't leave her in the house. She gets . . . um, lonely.'

Reverend Stowe scratched his head. 'There's a saying,' he said eventually. 'Ask no questions and you'll be told no lies. I wouldn't want anyone to have to lie in a house of God.' He clapped his hands, suddenly brisk and businesslike. 'So, you want to see the parish records. Births, marriages, deaths, that sort of thing. We have records going back several hundred years in the church office. I'll just leave you alone with the books while I make some tea, shall I?'

'Why do people keep wanting to make tea?' Howell asked after Reverend Stowe had bustled away, leaving them in the office with a stack of dusty books, a tea tray and an open tin of biscuits. 'It doesn't even taste nice.'

Ava took the first book off the pile. 'It's polite, and it makes us feel useful when we don't know what else to do.' She remembered what that was like from the weeks after her parents' death. She'd lost count of the cups of tea she'd made then.

'Ava, you can pour the tea,' Charles instructed. 'Everyone take a book each. Start with the newest ones and work back. We're looking for any reference to the Skinner family.'

Ava slapped her book back down. It had been *her* idea to come here, not Charles's, and now he was taking over.

Howell looked up at her and grimaced to show he understood, but Charles already had his head in a book and didn't notice.

'It doesn't matter who does what,' Lunette said quietly. 'We're a team.'

Ava didn't remember agreeing to be on a team with Charles, but for the next hour they all read in near silence. Matthew skimmed through pages, running his finger down each column. Howell and Lunette read more slowly, and Charles would have been quicker, but he kept looking over their shoulders to see if they'd found anything.

Ava mouthed some of the names as she read. Footer, Brown, Jones, Cowden. But not a single Skinner.

Three full pots of tea later, they'd gone through all the registers and they'd found nothing. Ava sighed as she stacked the registers back in the cupboard.

'It was a good idea,' Charles said.

'I know it was a good idea. A whole family couldn't live here and not have anyone get married or have children.'

'Or die,' Charles said.

Ava froze with her hand on the last book. 'Charles, you're a genius.'

*

147

Reverend Stowe was playing the organ again when they left. He paused to walk them to the door. The churchyard looked more autumnal than ever with threads of mist weaving between the gravestones. Ava wrapped her arms round herself and shivered as a cold breeze caught her.

'May we look around the churchyard on the way out?'

'Yes, of course.' Reverend Stowe loitered in the doorway, looking at Lunette and Howell as if he wanted to say something, but didn't know where to start. 'Some people fear the unknown,' he said at last. 'But in the end it's always better to be shaped by our kindness than our fear.' He shook hands with Lunette. 'I hope you enjoy the rest of your stay and get home safely. To Cambridgeshire, I mean, of course.'

'Why was he helping us?' Howell asked Ava.

She adjusted her coat and wrapped Mrs Footer's lead back round her hand. 'I don't know. I think he's just a nice man.' She headed down the path between the gravestones, pausing to look at each one. She was still irritated at Charles taking over the investigation. 'Sometimes, people are nice in this world.'

'I didn't say they weren't.'

His voice cracked on the last word. 'What's wrong?' Ava asked.

'Nothing.' He sat down heavily on a gravestone.

'You saw the skeleton, didn't you? It was horrible. What if it goes after Master Tudur? He hasn't done anything wrong. He's probably worrying about me right now. I was happy enough working in the House of Forgotten Mirrors. It wasn't the best job, but it was better than Waxing Gibbous. And now I'm stuck here in your world with no idea what's happening back home. I don't even know whether it'll ever be safe to return.'

It was the most Ava had heard him say in one go. 'I'm sorry,' she said. 'I didn't think.' She really hadn't. She'd thought it was bad moving from Cambridgeshire to Wyse, but at least she was in the same world.

'You'll go back,' she said. 'We'll find out what's going on, we'll save the covenant and the two worlds.'

Saving the covenant, however, didn't seem the best thing for the Unworld when it meant they had to keep producing enchantments for the human world.

'Ava,' Charles called.

She waved to show she'd heard him. 'Don't worry,' she said to Howell. 'We'll sort all this out.'

Howell raised his head. 'How?'

Ava didn't know what to say to that. Fortunately, Charles shouted again.

'Come on,' she said, and hurried across, towing Mrs Footer behind.

A red frog hopped across the path, followed by a squirrel – at least, Ava thought it was a squirrel.

It moved too quickly and all she saw was the tip of an orange tail vanishing up a tree. A bird shrieked, sounding almost human.

Charles stood in front of a gravestone so old that the writing was barely legible. The other stones in this patch were all overgrown and covered with moss, but this stone was clean, the grass around it was neatly trimmed. And a small vase of white flowers stood in front of it.

Ava crouched to read the inscription.

Mr Ephraim Skinner
1562–1602
And his wife Abigail
1570–1602
Much loved father and mother

Mr Skinner, not Lord Skinner.

'Lord Skinner's first name is Ephraim, isn't it?' she said. She sat back on her heels, gazing at the cold stone.

'They both died young,' Lunette said. 'Poor things.'

Younger than her own parents, Ava thought, and so long ago that the dates were almost meaningless to her – but not meaningless to whoever tended this grave. She bent to look closer at the writing beneath the two names and a shock of cold went through her.

Usually, gravestones had some verse from the Bible. This one had a verse, but she was sure it didn't come from the Bible.

When you're angry, when you're sad,
Put it in the mirror and you won't feel so bad.

CHAPTER 19

Is anyone even listening to me? No? Didn't think so.

Park Road, Wyse. Mist brushes across a flower bed and all the roses turn bright green.

New Theatre Street. A cat tears down the street at high speed, followed by another. And another. And another. Cats can usually tell when something is wrong.

Really, you need to start paying attention.

The Book

They walked back along the main streets. Being Sunday, all the shops were shut, and only a few groups of holidaymakers were strolling, complaining about the weather. Mist in July when it should have been bright sunshine.

Ava paused to let Mrs Footer sniff a lamp post. '*When you're angry, when you're sad . . .* I'd never heard of that poem before we came to Wyse,' she said, 'now it seems to be everywhere.'

'It's an odd choice for a gravestone,' Charles agreed. He wrote as he walked, and occasionally stopped to pick something up from the ground and examine it before throwing it away. 'The stone said *father and mother*. That means there must have been children. I wonder what happened to them?'

Ava stepped to one side to avoid a group of ladies in a shimmering rainbow of dresses. Matthew raised his hat to them.

'We're visiting from Cambridge,' Lunette said brightly. 'It rains a lot.'

The ladies gave her odd looks and walked on.

Lunette stopped outside a shop window. 'I never knew people needed so many teapots and tiny mirrors.'

'They don't,' Charles said, stopping beside her. 'Holidaymakers buy them because they're enchanted. But, of course, magic only works in Wyse, so, as soon as they leave, their souvenirs go back to being ordinary teapots and mirrors.'

'If they're lucky,' Howell said. 'We use all sorts of rubbish in our enchanted goods. Roses from dead leaves, food made from . . .' He broke off with a quick grimace. 'No, you probably don't want to know how enchanted food is made.' He studied the window, frowning. 'Charles, Ava, how many of these shops do you have?'

Charles counted on his fingers. 'Eight. Nine if you count the tourist information office.'

'That can't be right.' Howell stared closer at the

window. 'We make enchantments by the thousand in Waxing Gibbous. Where do they all go, if they don't come to your shops?'

'They don't go anywhere else,' Charles sighed. 'Like I said, enchantments don't work outside Wyse.'

Ava watched her breath turn to mist on the shop window. 'But if you're making all those enchantments in Unwyse, and only a small number make it into the shops here . . .'

'What's happening to the rest of them?' finished Matthew.

They were no closer to finding answers the next morning as Ava prepared to go to the Footers' house to work. She dressed slowly, her stomach churning with nerves at the thought of facing Mr Footer. Worse still, though, was the prospect of Matthew going to Waning Crescent. When she thought of him alone with Lord Skinner, her skin crawled.

'Any advice, Book?' she asked.

A few pale words appeared. *Don't go through strange doors.*

Not exactly useful.

Matthew pulled his tie straight. 'We'll be fine. We have to carry on as normal or people will wonder.'

Ava didn't care if people wondered. 'I'll go to work. You stay here.'

'And have Lord Skinner come here looking for me?'

Matthew put his hands on Ava's shoulders and gazed down at her, his face serious. 'I'll be careful, I promise.' He turned to Lunette, his expression softening. 'I'm sorry we have to leave you. Stay in the house, don't answer the door to anyone and we'll return as soon as we can.'

Lunette nodded. Unlike Howell, she didn't appear too worried, or maybe she was just covering it up better. 'We'll be fine,' she said. She put a grey top hat on Matthew's head. 'A protection hat. It will help a little.'

'And whatever Lord Skinner says, remember to believe the opposite,' Ava warned.

Outside, mist swallowed up the pale sunshine, turning the garden into a chilly, grey blur and the air smelled like burning toast. Only a few people were out and they all seemed on edge, hurrying on by with their heads down. A few times Ava heard rustlings in hedges, and as they passed one house a lady was screaming about fairies stealing the cheese.

Ava arrived at the Footers' house late and out of breath, wondering whether Mr Footer would let her in. She needn't have worried because she found the front door open. Three women were giving their sympathies to Mr Footer in the parlour while another two argued over casseroles in the kitchen. Ava hadn't realized her cousin was so popular. None of them paid any attention as Ava crept past. She was going to have to wait to speak to Mr Footer.

The thought made her heart bump nervously because she knew exactly what she was going to do while she was waiting. Stepping carefully and hoping no one would hear, she crept up the stairs to the room she'd been forbidden ever to enter: Mr Footer's study.

The murmur of voices continued downstairs.

Don't go through strange doors, The Book had said. Ava smoothed down her apron and straightened her shoulders. She was The Book's guardian, not its servant. She didn't have to do everything it said. Holding her breath, she pushed the study door open.

The room didn't look that much different from her father's study back home. A selection of comfortable chairs stood around one wall. Bookshelves. A desk, overflowing with papers, under the window, where a faint haze of mist drifted. And, against the opposite wall, a large, elaborately carved cabinet looked awkwardly out of place, its doors closed, a key in the burnished lock.

Ava's heart beat fast.

Father's mirror: it had to be. She walked across to the cabinet and gripped the key. It felt warm, as if someone had handled it recently. Ava started to turn it and paused. This was a proper, licensed working mirror, she thought, which meant its pair was in the Mirror Station in Unwyse. If she tried to use it, she might find herself face to face with Mr Bones.

She stood for a moment, her fingers still on the key, then, slowly, she let her hand fall. *Coward*, she chided herself silently.

She stepped back, and went to the desk instead. It looked like Mr Footer never tidied up after himself: empty envelopes, letters and bills all lay together. Ava started sorting through them, her hands still trembling slightly. Requests for private audiences, a letter of complaint from one family who'd ordered an enchanted puppy and hadn't expected it to turn into a pile of twigs after a week.

Then Ava recognized the precisely curved handwriting of Lord Skinner on an envelope.

She stopped still, finding it hard to breathe. The mist that crept through the window smelled of damp leaves.

Orders for Unwyse, she read. *Mr Footer, at the stroke of midnight when everyone is asleep, you will unlock your mirror and summon your fairy servant. When she appears, instruct her to make sure no one is listening. Then, when she confirms that this is done, please read the following paragraph.*

The following paragraph was brief. *Say: 'Mr Bones is looking for something. Find out what it is. Do not tell anyone what you are doing – especially not Mr Bones. You are ordered to keep this a secret. I will contact you again this time next week for your news.'*

Ava turned the paper over.

Your fairy servant will agree. Open your mirror again exactly one week from that time and write down what she says. Needless to say, this is a private matter and must be kept between the two of us. Destroy this letter once you have carried out the instructions.

Ava rested both hands on the desk, her head swimming. Lord Skinner was using Mr Footer to spy on Unwyse. Somehow, she wasn't surprised, but why do it in such a complicated fashion? And, clearly, Mr Footer had disobeyed Lord Skinner's instruction to destroy the letter. Why was that?

Ava searched the rest of the papers, and found more letters from him. Some asked for general news about Unwyse, but most of them mentioned Mr Bones. Then Ava unfolded the last one, right at the bottom of the pile. Underneath the usual instructions about secrecy, two sentences stood out: *Ten years ago, an enchantment was cast, magic taken from a boy. What happened to him?*

Ava froze, holding the paper in her hand. Downstairs a door opened. Voices and then silence. Still, Ava didn't move.

A boy – Howell. It had to be. Magic taken from a boy . . . but Howell said he didn't have any magic.

'What in blazes are you doing?' a voice demanded from the door.

Ava stuffed the paper into her apron pocket and spun round, hot embarrassment flooding her cheeks.

She'd never seen Mr Footer angry before. 'My mother told you never to come in this room,' he said, his moustache quivering. 'She hasn't been gone a day and you're already snooping.'

'I'm not snooping, I'm cleaning.' Ava tried to straighten the heap of letters behind her without him noticing. 'Mr Footer, I know where your mother is. She was accidentally enchanted. You saw her – the dog.'

Mr Footer's face turned crimson. 'I know how fairy magic works and it can't turn people into dogs. Get out.'

'No,' Ava said. She gripped the desk, surprised by her own boldness. Mr Footer goggled at her.

'Lord Skinner was using you to send secret messages to Unwyse,' Ava said. 'Why did you keep the letters? Did you forget to get rid of them? Or did you want to keep them as evidence – because, if you think about it really hard, you know Lord Skinner isn't really a fine gentleman.'

Something inside her hoped Mr Footer would suddenly see the truth, but she should have known it wouldn't be that easy.

'Just who do you think you are,' he barked, 'coming into my house and going through my private things?'

A stair creaked outside. 'Mr Footer? Is everything all right?'

'Yes, perfectly fine, thank you.' He turned back to Ava. 'You can take your things and leave,' he said. His voice was low and trembling. 'And tell your brother that this is my house now, and neither of you are welcome in it.'

CHAPTER 20

In the souvenir shop, a family of china mice come to life as mist curls around them. They scamper blindly from shelf to shelf as women screech, then one of them falls off and smashes on the floor.

Still not listening? Maybe you'll pay attention to this . . .

The Book

Will Gosling, chief apprentice at the House of Forgotten Mirrors, slouched through the streets on his way to work. He'd been away since Saturday evening. After the argument with Howell Fletcher on Saturday, Will hadn't felt like staying. He'd gone home for a bit and then when his mother had shooed him out he'd hung about with friends. Nobody came looking for him, which was fine at first, but slowly his annoyance grew. Didn't Master Tudur even care where he was? Or had Howell made up some story to get him into even more trouble?

Now it was Monday morning and he couldn't put off going back to work any longer. He slouched along the roads, inventing new arguments to start with Howell, new ways of making him sorry.

He shoved through the doors of the House of Forgotten Mirrors and stopped dead.

A station guard in a red uniform sat at the front desk. All around, sheets hung in crumpled folds over the many mirrors, as if they'd all been pulled off and replaced too hastily. And the mist. It crawled in thick folds across the floor, changing colour from grey to red to bright silver. All of it creeping towards one mirror that stood shrouded like all the rest, but the sheet moved gently in and out, almost as if something behind it was breathing.

'What's going on?' Will asked.

A dry, thin voice answered him. 'Are you Will Gosling?'

Will yelped.

Mr Bones stepped out of the doorway that led upstairs.

Will stumbled back, bumping against the door, his heart hammering hard enough to send pulses of hot colour to his cheeks.

'Come here,' Mr Bones ordered.

Will considered running, but something in Mr Bones's voice compelled him forward.

Mr Bones peeled his gloves off, then removed his hat and put the gloves neatly inside it. The whole thing took him about half a minute. 'Boy, are you loyal to Unwyse?' he asked.

Will felt sweat trickling down his back. He couldn't take his eyes off the empty gloves dangling their fingers over the brim. He tried to speak, but his voice dried up completely. All he could manage was a faint squeak and a jerky nod.

It seemed to be enough to satisfy Mr Bones, who nodded in return. 'We are investigating a recent sabotage attempt by anti-humanists. Master Tudur has been arrested. Your fellow apprentice – Howell Fletcher, I believe? – has fled. Have you seen him?'

Will shook his head dumbly. 'I haven't seen Howell since Saturday. I thought he was here.' His legs began to shake. Master Tudur arrested? Howell wanted for sabotage? Will pictured himself dragged off to Waxing Gibbous as a traitor and more sweat cascaded down his back.

'I'm not an anti-humanist,' he gulped. 'I'm loyal to Unwyse. I don't know about Master Tudur, but I've never liked Howell Fletcher. He was always sneaking out when he should have been working.'

Mr Bones ran his fingers round the brim of his hat. 'Very well, this is what will happen. You will go upstairs to your bed and pull your blanket over your head. You will stay there until called. Then you will keep watch here. If any of these mirrors show signs of life, or if Howell Fletcher comes back, you will report it straight to the station guards. But not that mirror.'

He pointed to the one surrounded by mist. 'You will stay well away from that one. Do not touch it. Do not even look at it. *Especially* do not look at it. Do you understand?'

Will slumped against the counter, giddy with relief. He didn't understand what was going on, only that he wasn't going to be arrested.

'Do you have paper?' Mr Bones asked.

Will nodded and pulled a sheet clumsily out of the desk drawer. Mr Bones wrote a single word on it. 'You can put that in the window,' he said, handing it to Will.

Will read it, his mouth dry.

Closed.

CHAPTER 21

If you're reading in bed, by the way, you should stop now. You don't want to give yourself nightmares. Or maybe you do – what would I know?

The Book

Matthew walked to Waning Crescent with a new sense of purpose on Monday morning. Mist clung to him, covering his coat with shimmering droplets, and the summer morning was quite unseasonably chilly, more like November than July.

The road lay quiet beneath ribbons of yellow mist. The iron gates at the end of the crescent stood open and the enchantments on the white stone buildings had an eerie glow. Matthew slowed, and for one moment he even considered turning round and running back home.

Ava's voice mocked him. *Where's your sense of adventure, Matthew?*

Matthew remembered all the times he'd said that to her while he stood by to see what would happen. He'd talked of adventure, but he'd never meant anything by it. Like a plain china jug enchanted to look like gold, he could put on a good show, but underneath it all he was dull, and, he suspected now, not especially brave.

He curled his hands into fists. Brave or not, he had to do this. He ran up the steps to the doors of Waning Crescent and rang the bell.

Lord Skinner opened the doors so quickly he must have been waiting behind them. 'Mr Harcourt. You're late.'

Matthew's thoughts scattered. He put a hand to his mouth and coughed. 'I apologize. I have the beginnings of a summer cold.' The many mirrors reflected his face, looking paler with each second.

'You certainly don't look well,' Lord Skinner agreed. 'You should come and sit down. Take off your hat. I'll order you some tea.'

He led the way along the hall. Matthew noticed again how he looked straight ahead as he strode past the mirrors, almost as if he was afraid of seeing himself in them.

'Why do you keep these mirrors?' Matthew asked. 'Couldn't you put them in storage?'

'I could. But what if one of them unexpectedly came to life, Mr Harcourt, and I didn't see it?' Lord Skinner turned suddenly to face him. 'What then?'

Matthew swayed. The hall blurred, the air suddenly smelling of must and old leaves. He squeezed his eyes shut, shaking his head in an effort to clear it. *Lord Skinner is not a fine gentleman*, he told himself.

He put a hand to Lunette's hat and his vision cleared. 'Now, look here, Lord Skinner,' he said, and he was pleased to note his voice only wobbled very slightly. 'I want to know what's going on. Who are you really, and what are you doing with these mirrors? I want to know the truth.'

Lord Skinner's faded eyes glittered menacingly. 'Are you sure about that, Mr Harcourt? I spent most of Saturday night convincing Mr Footer not to use his mirror. This morning I must talk to the rest of the conjurors, and then the rest of the town, no doubt. We are in the middle of a magical crisis and I have to fix it. And now you come here demanding answers.'

Matthew took a step backwards. 'On second thoughts, I think I should go home.'

'Don't you know it's bad manners to wear a hat indoors?' Lord Skinner said. He reached out, and before Matthew could stop him he plucked the hat from Matthew's head. Matthew's vision swam again. That smell. He gasped.

'You don't look well at all, Mr Harcourt,' Lord Skinner said, his voice suddenly sharp-edged. 'Why don't you come and sit down, and tell me everything you know.'

Matthew nodded and groped his way along the wall. He really did need to sit down.

*

'. . . Some tea, Mr Harcourt.'

Matthew groaned and opened his eyes. He was sitting in his chair at his desk at Waning Crescent. Lord Skinner bent over him, holding out a china cup.

'What happened?' Matthew asked. His head throbbed with a sick ache.

'You were taken ill,' Lord Skinner said. 'You're feeling much better now.'

Matthew's head began to clear. He took the tea and choked down a mouthful. Something had happened, he was sure of it. Why couldn't he remember?

Lord Skinner stood back. 'Don't worry, Mr Harcourt. There's been a little trouble, but I'm taking care of it. He checked his pocket watch. 'Speaking of which, I'm overdue for a meeting. You should stay here and rest. I'll ask one of the servants to look in on you.'

Matthew tried to stand up, but his legs wouldn't hold him. 'Where is Ava?' He had some dreadful feeling she was in trouble though he couldn't think how or why.

'I'll take care of your sister,' Lord Skinner promised with an odd smile. 'No doubt she'll join us here soon.' He went to the door. 'Please wait here, and don't worry.'

Matthew slumped back in his chair. Thank goodness Lord Skinner was here. He'd take care of everything. He was a fine gentleman.

CHAPTER 22

Don't walk through strange doors. Don't walk in the mist. Don't walk alone. Please note, fairy magic is not guaranteed to work as expected. Your level of personal danger may go up as well as down.

The Book

Ava slammed the front door of the Footers' house behind her. 'Lord Skinner is not a fine gentleman!' she shouted. The letter she'd stolen from Mr Footer's desk crinkled accusingly in her pocket.

An enchantment was cast, magic taken. She didn't know what it meant, but a feeling settled over her as if she'd swallowed a block of ice. She glared at the Footers' door again, then she stamped up the path and slammed the garden gate too.

The mist floated restlessly, smelling of oranges and lemons. A cat dashed across the road, chased by a blackbird. On the high street, the Wyse Emporium was closed, a notice in the window apologizing for 'unforeseen circumstances'. A family emerged from another shop in a rush. 'You don't want to go in there,' the man said. 'The teapots started singing and then attacked us.'

Ava looked into the shop. The floor was covered in broken china and the shop boy was staring at it all, looking as if he was waking from a bad dream.

'We're closing,' he said. 'Everyone is. Lord Skinner's orders.'

Ava backed out quickly. Mist swirled in her face, making it impossible to see properly. As she hurried away from the shop, she heard a faint sound. The back of her neck prickled.

Someone was watching her, she thought. She turned quickly, but she couldn't see anyone. The angry family had already gone into another shop, no doubt to tell everyone about their teapot ordeal.

Was that the crunch of a footstep?

Ava tensed. 'I know you're there,' she said loudly, hoping no one would answer. Nobody did, but her breath continued to thud in and out of her chest. A shower of leaves fell on her bonnet and she cried out in fright. The leaves turned into feathers, then melted back into mist.

She forced herself to laugh, but the sound came out slightly crooked, like someone who was only pretending to be brave and not doing it very well.

'Charles, if you're playing games,' she said, 'I'm going to be so cross with you.'

The mist hung still.

Ava put her hand to her cheek, feeling the cold crescent of the measles mark. She was being silly; no one was there. She should get back home and tell the others about Mr Footer and Lord Skinner.

She started to walk, faster than usual.

And then, right in front of her, the mist parted, leaving a clear space, and a figure stepped out.

Not Charles. A man, taller than Charles and thinner, with orange hair and ears that swept up into elegant points.

'They won't see me unless I want them to,' the Unworld man said, gesturing at the shop windows. 'It's my magic, so no one's going to come running to help you.'

Ava backed away. 'Who are you? Who invited you here?'

The Unworld man matched her, step for step. 'No one invited me. Someone left a door open between our worlds. Magic is leaking through and where magic comes we can find a way. I've been sent to find something. Two criminals from our world stole an item and fled here with it. A book.'

Ava tried not to react, but she couldn't help herself. The Unworld man's lips curved slyly. 'You know where it is, don't you . . . Ava Harcourt?'

She jumped. 'How do you know who I am?'

'I've been listening to people. They talk a lot

around here, don't they? A young girl with a mark on her cheek, and her brother.' He started faster through the mist towards her, his feet making no sound on the cobbles. 'Tell me where Howell Fletcher is.' He reached out his hand to her.

'Help!' Ava screamed. 'Fairies!'

People might not be able to see the Unworld man, but they could hear Ava. Doors opened.

'Someone's there,' a shopkeeper said. 'In the mist.'

That wiped the smile off the Unworld man's face. Magic didn't work so well on this side of the mirror, Ava thought. He hadn't expected that!

'Get him!' she cried, and she ran. She heard people shouting behind her. Maybe they'd caught the Unworld man, maybe not, but she didn't wait to find out. The bakery – Charles would be there. Which way was it? All the narrow roads suddenly looked alike in the mist.

The theatre loomed out, directly ahead. Ava almost fell over a pair of boards advertising that day's shows. Cursing the mist, she ran on, down the road to the left, and wrenched at the bakery door.

It didn't open.

Ava hammered on the glass. 'Charles! Charles, let me in.' Her sides heaved, and then, through the sound of her own laboured breathing, she heard footsteps.

'Where is Howell Fletcher?' the Unworld man asked. He paused at the top of the road, his arms folded, head tilted to one side, looking as if this was a game he was enjoying playing.

There was no point running. He was faster than her: he'd catch her before she'd gone twenty paces.

Ava ran anyway. She heard him behind her and she kept going. She was almost at the church now. If she could get inside, she could lock the door against him.

Something moved ahead of her. Not something – people. Two people.

'Ava!' Lunette shouted. 'Duck!'

Ava ducked as Lunette threw a hat, then she watched open-mouthed as it stretched out into the shape of a duck in flight and swooped straight into the Unworld man's face and wrapped around his head.

He gave a muffled shout and tried to tear it off.

'My hat of not-seeing,' Lunette said. 'It won't last long. The Book told us to find you near the church.'

'The Book did something useful?' Ava looked at the fairy man staggering as he tried to tear the feathered hat from his face. A wash of tiredness swept over her.

'Charles's house is closest,' Howell said. 'Do you want to . . .'

Ava shook her head. They'd caused the Brunel family enough trouble already. 'Let's just go home.'

My pages itch. You should clean your bag sometime. There are more than 35,000 species of spider in the human world. Some of the spiders eat paper.

'Never mind spiders,' Ava said. She sat at the kitchen table, still feeling shaky. Howell put a cup of tea in front of her while Lunette checked all the doors and windows were locked. Mrs Footer lay across the back door, growling softly.

They couldn't stay here, Ava thought. The Unworld man would come looking for them, and Matthew was still stuck at Waning Crescent.

The Book's pages stirred again. *Magic is attracted to this world. It belongs here, after all, and it wants to come back. The mirrors act as a barrier and prevent it coming through, but now a mirror is broken. This is what happens when you leave a door open.*

Howell added salt to his tea. 'You mean this is our fault.'

Outside, a bird flew by, backwards.

'It's my fault,' Ava said. 'I broke the mirror in the Footers' parlour.'

'Only because I told you to,' Howell said. 'Book, how do we stop it?'

You sever the connection, obviously.

Yes, obviously. Ava sighed. 'Sever the connection. Right. Any hints?'

I'm a book of prophecy, not an instruction manual. You could drain all the magic from the connection. Or break the other mirror. That will work too.

But the other mirror was in Unwyse, Ava thought.

She dug in her apron pocket for the folded piece of notepaper.

'*Magic taken from a boy,*' Howell read. 'What does that mean?'

'I hoped you might know. Lord Skinner has been spying on Unwyse for a while, I think.' She buried her head in her hands. 'And he's not the only one spying. Mr Bones is getting closer too. That man said "we". He *said*, "where magic comes through, we can find a way." There are more of them. We're surrounded!'

CHAPTER 23

The British are known all over the world for their politeness and for their obedience to the rules. They even invent new games just so they can have fun playing by the rules and generally being beaten.

Magic also follows rules. It's just that you people don't know what the rules are.

The Book

Matthew sat alone, his eyes half closed, waiting for the walls to stop spinning. Something didn't seem quite right. He'd been taken ill – he could believe that – but before that there'd been something else, something he couldn't quite remember. *Reflections bouncing about the grand hallway; Lord Skinner talking, asking questions.*

Matthew pushed himself to his feet. A servant looked around the open doorway so quickly that Matthew suspected the man must have been standing guard outside.

'I'm fine,' Matthew croaked. 'Maybe a glass of water?'

The servant nodded and withdrew.

Matthew started to sag back into the chair, but stopped himself. Words echoed in his ears as if he was remembering them from a long time ago. *Tell me the truth, Mr Harcourt.*

And his own voice, mumbling answers, telling Lord Skinner everything – Ava, Howell, the mirror, The Book, all of it.

A surge of panic drove the rest of the fog from his mind. Lord Skinner knew. Matthew had to find Ava and warn her. He stumbled to the door and looked out. The servant emerged from the direction of the kitchen, carrying a glass of water on a tray. He paused when he saw Matthew.

'Here's your water, sir,' he said. 'You should sit back down and wait for Lord Skinner. He's a fine gentleman.'

No, he wasn't. Whatever Lord Skinner was, he was *not* a fine gentleman.

Matthew reached for the glass, lifted it up and threw the contents into the servant's face. Then he ran.

The servant shouted behind him. Other servants appeared through doorways. Matthew dodged them all, shoved one out of the way, and tore open the doors of Waning Crescent. With angry shouts following him, he rushed out into the mist.

He didn't stop running until he reached the end of the crescent and was sure no one was chasing him. He slowed, breathing hard.

Funny: he felt he could see more clearly now he was out of Lord Skinner's home, even though the mist was heavier than ever.

At least the mist meant anyone looking for him would have trouble seeing him. He walked quickly away from Waning Crescent. To the Footers' house first, he thought. Find Ava, and then they could decide what to do.

He was approaching the theatre in the middle of town when the mist parted and he caught a glimpse of a red jacket.

'Hello?' Matthew called, taking an uncertain step forward. Another flash of red in the mist.

A hand touched his shoulder from behind.

'What are we going to do?' Ava asked.

Howell couldn't bring himself to look at her. He'd thought he'd escaped Mr Bones when he'd fled through the mirror; instead, he'd only put Ava and Matthew in danger too.

'I'm sure we can find a way out of this,' Lunette said.

Howell nodded, but only because he wanted her to be quiet for a moment. Mr Bones could find them even here. If they hadn't found Ava in time . . . No, he didn't want to think what might have happened to Ava if they hadn't found her in time.

Then someone banged on the kitchen window. Howell jumped up with a yell of fright.

'Did I scare you?' Charles asked, opening the door.

Howell sank back down, his heart racing. 'No.' He tried to smile. 'You scared Ava half to death, though. Where have you been?'

'At home. Lord Skinner has been telling everyone to stay indoors and Mum believed him. She still thinks he's a fine gentleman.' Charles grimaced. 'Lord Skinner might have a point for once, actually – the mist is getting worse.'

It was getting more like Unwyse, Howell thought.

Ava got up and put the kettle on the stove, her hands shaking. 'Were you followed?' she asked Charles.

'Not that I noticed. And I probably would. What's going on?'

'It's my fault,' Howell said. 'I told Ava to break the Footers' mirror and now there's a broken magical connection leaking magic into Wyse. The only way to stop it is to break the mirror it's paired with. Which is in Unwyse,' he added.

Charles nodded and sat down. 'So how do we get to Unwyse to break the mirror?'

Howell sighed. 'You don't. I do.' He held up his hand as Charles started to argue and Ava turned round. 'You don't know what it's like in Unwyse. I do. I have to go back.'

He wasn't exactly sure how he'd do it, but if Mr Bones could send guards to Wyse, there must be a way back too. If only he knew what it was.

The Book stirred, a page turning over slowly.

'Does everything written in that book really come true?' Charles asked. 'What if I wrote that I found a pile of treasure in my back garden?'

You can't write in me, Charles Brunel. Matthew Harcourt is feeling unwell. He thinks Lord Skinner is a fine gentleman.

Howell felt a jolt of panic go through him. Behind him, Ava dropped a teacup. 'Matthew!'

Hot tea splashed Howell's feet. He slammed The Book shut and jumped up. 'Ava, wait a moment.'

She looked down at the broken bits of cup and the spreading puddle, her face white and pinched. 'I knew I shouldn't have let him go off alone.' She snatched up her bonnet and crammed it on to her head.

Howell caught her arm. 'Ava, please wait.'

'You wait here if you want,' she said. 'I'm going to Waning Crescent.'

'I just meant we'll all go,' Howell said. His heartbeat drummed in his ears. He looked at the mist swirling at the windowpanes. How many of Mr Bones's people were out there?

*

The mist curled into menacing shapes as they hurried in the direction of Waning Crescent. Ghostly hands snatched at them and melted away again. Grinning skull faces appeared and disappeared. A bush waved its branches threateningly, then tried to grab Mrs Footer. Howell pulled her out of the way and kicked the bush. Wyse was becoming more like Unwyse all the time.

Ava and Charles stumbled along. The mist bothered them far more than him and Lunette, Howell thought. Maybe their human eyes weren't used to it.

'It'll be fine,' he said, trying to convince himself it was true. 'We'll find Matthew, then Lunette and I will go back to Unwyse. Once The Book is back there, Mr Bones will leave you alone.'

'But I'm The Book's guardian too,' Ava protested. 'I want to help. Anyway, you don't even know how to get home.'

'I'll work it out.'

Somehow, the mist made him feel more at home and less terrified. And knowing that he couldn't escape Mr Bones helped in some strange way. There was no point in running away, so he had to go back to Unwyse.

'Let's rescue Matthew first and worry about The Book later,' Lunette said firmly.

Howell was surprised at how fierce she looked. He knew she liked Matthew, but he hadn't previously known her to put anything or anyone before The Book. Even when the skeleton had attacked them in the House of Forgotten Mirrors, her first thought had been to protect The Book. Could she and Matthew be forming a connection of their own? he wondered.

They hurried on. There was no sign of the Unworld guard by the church, although duck feathers from Lunette's hat lay all over the ground. She gathered a few of them up. 'That's another hat that won't be growing back for a while,' she said with a sigh.

Mrs Footer lagged behind, snapping at the remaining feathers. Howell picked her up. Strange that he wasn't afraid of dogs any more either, and stranger still that Mrs Footer curled up against him with a sigh as if resigned to the fact that she couldn't do anything.

The town centre was deserted. Every shop had a 'closed' notice, and several had an additional notice.

On the advice of Lord Skinner, this shop is shut until further notice. We apologize for the inconvenience.

Outside the theatre, a sign announced that all conjuring shows had been cancelled due to unforeseen circumstances, but that the Wyse Town Dramatic Society was performing excerpts from Shakespeare instead.

And then Howell saw a flash of red through the mist.

'Matthew!' Ava cried.

Howell saw him a moment later. He was struggling against two Unworld guards – an orange-haired man and another one whom Howell recognized at once. He stopped dead. 'Luel.'

Luel turned to him and smiled. 'Hello, Howell. I made it to the human world, after all.'

'Let my brother go,' Ava shouted.

Luel cast her an indifferent glance. 'Certainly. As soon as your friends give us the book they stole.'

'We didn't steal it,' Howell said.

'Didn't you? Well, Mr Bones wants it anyway. Sorry – we're just following orders.'

Ava started forward. Charles caught hold of her arm to stop her as Lunette reached into her bag for a hat.

'I wouldn't do that,' the orange-haired guard said to her. He walked backwards, dragging Matthew with him, and they both appeared to fade slightly as if they were now only half in this world. 'Mr Bones wants you and Howell, and the book you're carrying. Come back to Unwyse with us and we'll let this human go. Otherwise, you'll never see him again.'

'Lunette, don't give them The Book,' Matthew said, his voice a croak.

Lunette closed her bag. 'Let him go. You don't need

Howell, either. I'll come with you.'

'No,' Howell said, but Lunette was already stepping away from him. He watched helplessly. She couldn't give herself up to Mr Bones. She just couldn't.

And then he heard the sound of a carriage approaching at speed. He jumped back out of the road as horses appeared, rearing up as the carriage slowed to a clumsy halt behind. Lord Skinner leaned out of the window.

'Begone,' he said, pointing a shaking finger at the Unworld guards. 'Go back to your own world.'

Nobody moved for a second. Howell hadn't seen Lord Skinner before and he stared at the sight of him. He didn't look quite human, his tall hat askew on his head, his eyes shining bright.

'Begone!' he shouted again.

Luel started to say something, but abruptly he and the other guard both vanished – and Matthew vanished with them.

'Matthew!' Ava shoved Charles away and ran to where the guards had been standing. 'Where have they gone?' she demanded.

'I sent them back to the Unworld,' Lord Skinner said calmly. 'The Fair Folk have to obey us, you know.'

That was a lie, Howell thought. The Unworld had to fulfil orders for magical services given through the mirrors, but that wasn't the same thing at all.

Yet, for some reason, the two guards *had* obeyed Lord Skinner. Why?

Lord Skinner opened the carriage door. 'You might show a little gratitude as I saved you from the same fate. Now, if you want to see your brother again, Miss Harcourt, I suggest you come with me – you and the boy. I have a job for you.'

CHAPTER 24

The Book apologizes for the lack of a witty header on this chapter. Normal service will resume soon. Possibly. Or possibly not. Probably not, actually, but don't let me worry you. I'm sure you have far more important things to worry about.

The Book

For a moment, Ava was filled with warm relief. All she had to do was tell Lord Skinner about Howell and Lunette and the mirrors, and he would sort everything out. She even started to walk towards the carriage.

Three sets of hands pulled her back, and one set of teeth, courtesy of Mrs Footer. Ava shook them all off.

'I'm fine,' she said. 'He can't trick me any more.' She straightened her shoulders and faced the carriage. the thoughts that invaded her mind were lies, she knew it. 'We're not going anywhere with you, Lord Skinner. You're a fraud. You might have fooled everyone else in this town, but you can't lie to me.'

'You can think what you like about me, Miss Harcourt,' Lord Skinner said testily, 'but I assure you Mr Bones is a thousand times worse. He will keep your brother out of spite and he'll never let him go, not even if you give him all the books in the world.' He took his hat off and rubbed at his scalp. His hair had bald patches that Ava hadn't noticed before. 'But,' he said. 'I can make him.'

Again, she had to fight against that sense of relief. Lord Skinner was all lies, but somehow this sounded like the truth. She glanced at the others and then the carriage driver, who sat like a rock, appearing oblivious to everything.

Lunette took a hat out of her bag. 'You can rescue Mr Harcourt? Then do so. Now.'

Lord Skinner's gaze sharpened. 'Threaten me, young lady, and you certainly won't see Matthew Harcourt again. The time has come for us to work together.'

'We're not giving you The Book,' Howell said.

'I don't want it.' An expansive shrug stretched Lord Skinner's waistcoat to breaking point. 'I must admit I'm intrigued as to why Mr Bones desires it so much,' he said, 'but as long as it doesn't fall into his hands you can keep it. I have something else in mind.' He turned back to Ava. 'The two of you opened a mirror that was supposed to be dead – brought it back to life. If you can do it once, you can do it again.'

'How do you know about that?' Ava asked.

A sly smile stole across Lord Skinner's face. Of course, Matthew would have told him. Matthew would have told him everything. Ava resisted the urge to stamp her foot. Why had she ever let Matthew go to Waning Crescent this morning?

'Come back to Waning Crescent with me,' Lord Skinner said. 'You don't need to revive every mirror there. Maybe a hundred to start with, and then we'll see about helping your brother.'

'Why don't you command Howell to do it?' Charles asked. 'You said Fair Folk have to obey.'

Why did Charles have to put that idea in Lord Skinner's mind? Ava tried to elbow him back.

'Yes, why don't you?' Howell asked.

Lord Skinner's face creased in irritation. 'Clearly, it's not quite that easy. I don't just need your co-operation, I need Miss Harcourt's as well.' He rubbed a hand over his eyes, suddenly looking tired. 'The two of you have a connection, you see, one that reaches between the worlds.'

He only knew that because Matthew had seen it in The Book and told him, Ava thought. And yet the way Lord Skinner was looking at her sent a prickle down her back: a knowing smile on his lips, and a vast hunger in his eyes.

Connected. She'd puzzled about that before, and now a horrible thought was unfurling in her mind that she tried to pretend wasn't there. It couldn't be true, because, if it was, it would mean she'd ruined another person's life.

Lord Skinner set his hat back on his head. 'I don't have all day. It's me or Mr Bones. Make up your minds.'

Put like that, what choice did they have? If it wasn't for her opening the mirror in the first place, none of this would have happened. She had to save Matthew, even if it meant opening every mirror in Waning Crescent.

But no: there was another way. It wasn't much better than the alternatives, but, if everything Lord Skinner said was true, it was possible.

'We need time to think,' she said. 'Meet us tonight at moonrise. In the churchyard – there's a gravestone for an Ephraim Skinner. You should know where it is.'

Was it her imagination or did Lord Skinner flinch at the mention of the gravestone? He nodded and touched the brim of his hat.

'An interesting choice. Very well. Moonrise. Naturally, I suggest you don't tell anyone else about this conversation. They wouldn't believe you.'

He closed the carriage door. A moment later, the driver shook the reins and the carriage moved away.

Howell turned on her at once. 'We are not going to open any mirrors for him.'

Ava ran her fingers under her bonnet ribbon. It felt too tight, cutting in uncomfortably. 'I know. We're going to open just one of them. While Lord Skinner is waiting for us in the churchyard, we'll break into Waning Crescent. Then we'll open a mirror, go to Unwyse and rescue Matthew ourselves.'

Charles dropped his notebook. Howell was already shaking his head. 'We don't even know it will work again.'

It would, Ava thought. It would, because they were connected. She suddenly found she couldn't look at Howell. 'You said all the dead mirrors are in the House of Forgotten Mirrors, didn't you?'

'Yes, but Mr Bones will be watching them by now.' He tried to pull her round to face him. 'What's wrong?'

She couldn't bear to see the worry in his eyes. She turned away, looking about the road for any sign of Unworld guards. She couldn't see any red jackets, but anyone might be listening. 'We should find somewhere to hide until moonrise,' she said.

Charles picked up Mrs Footer. 'My house is closest.' He gave Ava a sharp glance, then hurried Howell along the road. Ava followed them, staying behind so she wouldn't have to talk to them. This was all her fault – all of it.

Lord Skinner rushed into Waning Crescent and ran up the stairs without pausing to put down his walking stick or take off his hat. His breath heaved as he fumbled with multiple sets of keys until, finally, he burst through the door into the room beyond.

As always, the stench of decay hit him first and he clapped a handkerchief to his nose as he turned to face a tall mirror that hung on the wall beside the door.

'I told you not to interfere,' he shouted. 'I *ordered* you not to. You can't come through without an invitation. How did you do it?'

The mirror clouded, then cleared to show a face that was not Lord Skinner's. The face stared at him, expressionless. 'A door is open between our worlds and you are not the only one with servants to do your bidding.'

Lord Skinner tightened his grip on his walking stick. If he could see his own face, he knew it would be white with fear. White and old.

'I don't know why you want this book,' he said, 'but you can't have it. You will withdraw all your people from Wyse and tell them to leave us alone.'

He raised his walking stick to the mirror.

The face in the mirror smiled. 'Go ahead if you've finished.'

Lord Skinner's hand shook. He tried to bring his stick down on to the glass, he even imagined the mirror breaking into a thousand pieces, but he couldn't make himself do it. Uttering a cry of frustration, he threw down his stick and ran from the room, trembling all over and gasping as if he'd been running.

He needed more magic. He was so tired, and the hunger threatened to turn him inside out. He stumbled down the stairs, forgetting completely to lock the door behind him.

CHAPTER 25

In the bakery, a pie is cut and magpies swoop out, then turn back into pastry.

A carriage driver notices his horses' tails are on fire. He runs away screaming, but the horses don't appear to mind.

The Book

Investigation Notes by Charles Brunel
1. Matthew has been taken by Unworld guards. Rescuing him is our priority.
2. Mr Bones wants The Book, for reasons unknown.
3. Lord Skinner wants Ava and Howell to bring the magic mirrors back to life. Investigations have failed to reveal anything about Lord Skinner's background apart from two ancestors who are buried in the churchyard.
4. Lord Skinner commanded the Unworld guards and they obeyed him. According to Howell and Lunette, this is not part of the magical covenant.
5. Howell and Ava have a magical connection. This also requires more investigation.

6. Large amounts of enchanted goods are created in Unwyse, far more than are actually sold or used in Wyse. What is happening to them all?

'Anything else?' Charles asked.

Ava sat on his bed. It felt odd to be here without Matthew. She tried not to think about what might be happening to him, but she couldn't help it. Matthew, locked up in an Unworld dungeon while Mr Bones threatened him. She shivered.

Charles made another note in his notebook. 'I still think you should tell my parents about this. They'll get Freedom for Fair Folk to help you.'

Ava shook her head fiercely. When they'd arrived at Charles's house, he'd told his mother Matthew was working late and the others needed somewhere safe to spend the night. Ava didn't like the lie, but it was better than admitting the truth. 'We need more evidence,' she said. 'That will be your job. Howell, Lunette and I will find Matthew and you will keep investigating here, and prove to everyone that Lord Skinner is a fraud,' she added.

Mrs Footer barked as if in agreement.

Ava looked at Howell, hunched on the other side of the bed with The Book open beside him.

If I were you, I'd worry less about talking and more about getting on with things, The Book wrote.

Remember Madame Brille. 77 Euphorbia Lane, Unwyse.

Ava's heart leaped. 'Is that where they've taken Matthew?'

'No, it's my aunt's house,' Lunette said. 'What does my aunt have to do with this?'

The light bulb will be invented in 1879 and the zip fastener in 1891. Both of these will be most useful. If the world continues.

Ava sighed and slid off the bed. 'We should be going.'

Charles didn't look any happier than the rest of them. 'All right. I'll tell Mum I'm making hot milk for you – that'll get her into the kitchen to supervise. I've found that if you're careful you can climb out of this window. Good luck.'

He clumped out of the room making far more noise than necessary. 'Mum! I'm going to warm some milk.'

Ava waited until she heard doors open and shut downstairs, then she opened the window. The ground seemed an awfully long way below her, but a tree grew alongside the window and she could grab one of its branches if she stretched. She took a deep breath. Matthew was depending on her. She reached out, just about caught the branch and swung down clumsily, skinning one hand and ripping her skirt, but landing safely.

'I wish I still had my attack hat,' Lunette muttered,

dropping down beside her.

Something scurried across the road, half hidden by mist, far too fast for Ava to make out what it was. The mist was growing heavier, almost blotting out the moonlight.

They set off, walking quickly, not talking until they reached the top of Waning Crescent. Fairy lanterns burned at intervals, turning the mist green. All the windows of the crescent were blank and dark.

'It looks like no one's home,' Howell said uncertainly.

Now that they were here, Ava felt sick with fear. She started trying the windows, one at a time. What if Lord Skinner's servants were still here, or if Lord Skinner came back too soon?

Howell walked past her, scanning the front of the building. He seemed to be able to see far better than her in this mist. He pushed at a window and it scraped open.

'It's empty,' he said, looking inside.

Then Lunette squeezed past and climbed through the window, landing with thump that made Ava wince.

After a moment, Howell shrugged. 'I guess it's safe.' He climbed in and offered Ava his hand.

Ava wiped her palms on her skirt and scrambled in. This was it. In a few minutes, if all went well, they'd be in Unwyse.

*

'This is like the House of Forgotten Mirrors,' Howell said, staring down the great hall.

Ava kept her gaze on the floor, avoiding looking at her own reflection. She didn't want to accidentally bring a mirror to life before they were ready.

Then Lunette nudged her. 'What's that?' she asked.

A golden rectangle of light glowed at the top of the stairs. It was the wrong colour for candlelight, and too steady. And, as Ava neared the staircase, she smelled that familiar odour of dead leaves and decay. It seemed to tumble down over her in waves, making her dizzy.

Lunette sniffed. 'What *is* that?' She started up the stairs. Pale shadows spread over the wall and Ava saw that, just ahead of her at the top of the stairs, a door stood open. The light was coming from behind it.

Howell ran up the stairs after Lunette. 'We don't have time for this. Lord Skinner will be back soon.' But then, as if drawn to the light at the top, he kept climbing past Lunette.

'Ava,' he said, his voice sounding strange. 'You should come and see this.'

'See what?' Ava asked. Her stomach knotted. What could Lord Skinner be hiding at the top of Waning Crescent? Various images ran through her mind, from a vast hoard of magic mirrors to a stash of dead bodies. She climbed the stairs after Howell and Lunette, curiosity warring with dread at what she might find.

At least there weren't any bodies. Instead, the room was knee-deep in mist and piled high on three sides with rubbish. Great heaps of it – dead branches, old sacks with leaves spilling out of them, tangled piles of rags, even a basket of what looked like very old bread, covered in green mould.

The smell of decay filled Ava's mouth and nose, half choking her as she walked past Howell into the room. Something flickered on the wall and she jumped, then she realized she'd seen her own reflection. A full-length mirror hung on the wall beside the door. The glass was covered in a fine layer of dust, and smeared as if someone had rubbed against it recently, and the frame was ornate, scrolls and leaves and flowers curling together, all of them glossy black.

They all stood and stared at it.

'Is it magic?' Ava asked, knowing already that it had to be. This was Lord Skinner's secret – he had his own mirror.

Howell picked up a dead rose and crumbled the stem between his fingers. 'This came from Unwyse. We wondered what happened to all the enchanted goods. Now we know. They all end up here. But what is Lord Skinner doing with them?'

Ava put her hand out to the mirror and drew back, not wanting to touch the glass in case it came to life.

'You said there are six active mirrors in the Mirror Station,' she said.

Howell nodded, crumbling another rose.

And they knew where the corresponding six mirrors in Wyse were – with the six conjurors. This mirror was not one of those. Ava spotted something long and dark on the floor: Lord Skinner's walking stick. She picked it up and ran her fingers across the smooth wood, frowning. It made even less sense that he should send messages to Unwyse through Mr Footer when he had his own mirror all along.

'Wherever this mirror leads, I doubt it's the Mirror Station,' Howell said unsteadily. 'Shall we try opening it to find out?'

Ava started to nod. She even started to raise her hand to the mirror's cold surface, but then a sudden surge of panic overwhelmed her. No: wherever this mirror led, she didn't want to end up there.

'Leave it alone,' she said. 'We should stick to our plan.'

She put the walking stick back on the floor and hurried out of the room. Back in the hall, mirror after mirror reflected her anxious face, the crescent on her cheek looking as if it had been burned there.

It was a shame they couldn't tell Charles about this, she thought – it could be the evidence he needed. They'd have to tell him later, if they made it back to Wyse.

'Which mirror should we try?' Howell asked.

Ava didn't know. If The Book was right, they should be able to open any one of them. And if she was right about why, she thought, Howell would never forgive her.

She took a deep breath, forcing the thought away. The only thing that mattered now was finding Matthew. She reached for the nearest mirror.

Nothing happened. The cold surface remained flat and glossy.

'Let's try this one,' Howell said, putting his hand on another one. Ava joined him and they both pushed the glass.

Still nothing. 'Please open,' Ava said. Her hand started to tremble. This wasn't working. They'd come here for nothing, Matthew was still trapped, and there was nothing she could do to help.

Click. The sound of a door opening.

Ava backed away into Howell, staring in dismay.

Lord Skinner took off his hat and smiled at her. It was an odd smile: dazed and a little dreamlike. 'Miss Harcourt and friends,' he said. 'I thought we were meeting at the churchyard. Never mind, you've saved me the trouble of searching for you.'

CHAPTER 26

There are many stories of humans who have strayed into the Unworld. Usually the stories end up with them going mad, or returning to their own world and finding that a hundred years have passed.

You'll be pleased to know this is unlikely to happen to you. The stories were invented to dissuade people from trying to cross the boundary into the Unworld. Human people cause enough chaos in their own world without inviting them into ours.

The Book

Howell couldn't move, not even when Ava backed into him. Lord Skinner stood at the end of the grand hall, one old man against the three of them. If they ran, Howell thought, he'd never be able to catch them. Howell tried to lift his feet, but they felt heavy as stone.

Lord Skinner is a fine gentleman. The thought buzzed quietly in his ears.

Ava trod on his foot. The pain jolted him back to

reality, which wasn't the most comforting place to be right now. He wet his lips.

'You're too late,' he said. 'We're leaving and you can't stop us.' His tongue felt too big for his mouth. 'We know what you're hiding – we found your mirror.'

Lord Skinner sighed and shook his head. Flaps of pale skin wobbled below his chin. 'Oh dear. Still, it was inevitable someone would eventually. I was only doing what all the shopkeepers and conjurors do in this town – bringing goods through from Unwyse. I need their magic, you see.'

'For what?' Ava demanded. She was pale. 'To make everyone like you – to think you're a fine gentleman?' She almost spat the last word.

Lord Skinner gave another shuddering sigh. 'Yes, there is that. But mainly just to stay alive. Please, come and sit down, and hear me out. I'll tell you the truth – all of it.'

More lies, Howell thought, but Lord Skinner didn't look as if he was lying. He looked sunken, half defeated.

Lunette was already reaching into her bag, ready to pull out a hat.

'You're young,' Lord Skinner said. 'You think you've got all the time in the world. Wait until you're in your sixth decade with only death ahead of you, and you haven't achieved half of what you want. Then you might understand. You ought to understand,

Miss Harcourt. You're alive because of magic.'

'What's he talking about?' Howell asked. He darted a glance at the nearest mirror. They might still be able to open it up and escape to Unwyse. But then he might never find out what was happening here, and suddenly he found he wanted to know, even if meant staying. He stepped away from the mirrors.

'I only meant to try it once,' Lord Skinner was saying. 'Just to gain a little more time. The magic that connects the mirrors is strong; I didn't think I'd need many. Each pair of mirrors gave me a few extra years. But the years were never long enough. There was always so much work to be done.'

Lunette froze, hat in hand, her blue eyes wide. 'You killed the mirrors.' Her voice shook. 'You stole their magic to keep yourself alive.'

Lord Skinner inclined his head. His eyes were rimmed with red and shadow. Beside Howell, Ava stood like stone. 'But the mirrors were dying in seventeen ten,' she said. 'You can't be that old.'

'Can't I?' Lord Skinner asked. He gestured to the door behind him. 'Please.'

Howell followed as Lord Skinner led them through a huge dining room into a kitchen that was five times the size of Ava's. The back door stood open and thin threads of mist crawled through, tangling around the pans on the kitchen wall. One of the pans began to twist, trying to escape from its hook.

'The gravestone . . .' Howell began.

'My parents. I was their only child. I was very fond of them though it was a long time ago.' Lord Skinner sat down, making the chair creak. 'Kitchens are such comforting places, don't you find?' His voice wavered. 'Do you know what it's like to be hungry – constantly, awfully hungry and no amount of food can fill the space inside you?'

Howell tried to imagine it. The closest he could come up with was his own lack of magic, but that seemed like nothing compared with the terrible emptiness in Lord Skinner's eyes.

'How?' he asked, fascinated and repulsed. 'How did you do it?'

'I discovered a way of drawing magic out of mirrors.' Lord Skinner's gaze drifted. 'The first time I did it, it felt like I'd been reborn. I thought once would be enough, but it wasn't. I did it again, and again. Finally, the mirrors started running out until there were only a handful left. I preserved them here, keeping watch over the conjurors who use them. I hid my own mirror and used it to bring magical goods from Unwyse. Those scraps of magic have been just enough to keep me alive.'

The pans on the wall hung still again, seeming too afraid to move.

An unnerving smile stretched Lord Skinner's lips.

'But now you can change everything. You can bring mirrors back to life. I will have unlimited connections to feed off, as much magic as I could ever need. And in return, Miss Harcourt, I will order Mr Bones to return your brother to you. I do have the power to do that.'

Howell shuddered. He didn't need The Book to tell him what would happen if they gave Lord Skinner what he wanted. There would be no end to it – Lord Skinner's hunger might be satisfied for a little while, but it would grow again until it consumed everything – not just Wyse and Unwyse but the whole world and Unworld with them. He curled his hands into fists. 'No,' he said. 'We won't do it.'

Lord Skinner's gaze snapped round to him. 'I'm afraid you must. Miss Harcourt, you already owe me your life. I remember the day your father came to me, needing more powerful magic than he could summon with his mirror. I gave him the books he needed, told him what to ask for. All I wanted in return was an occasional message passed through his mirror.'

Ava shook her head, her face drawn tight.

'What magic?' Howell asked her, extending his hand to her.

She pushed it away. 'There's no magic. My parents moved to get away from magic. Father told me to stay away from mirrors. It was the last thing he said before he died.'

Ava's parents were dead? 'I'm sorry,' he began,

the words sticking in his throat. 'I thought they were travelling or something, like mine.' No wonder she looked so sad sometimes. He reached out to her again but she shrugged him away without looking at him.

'I lost my parents when I was a child too,' Lord Skinner said softly. 'Cholera. Very few people survived. I know what it's like to grow up alone, with only myself for company. You and I are similar in many ways, Miss Harcourt.'

Ava shook her head. 'I'm not alone. I have Matthew.'

'And what does Matthew think about that?' Lord Skinner asked.

Ava didn't answer, but her cheeks reddened.

Strands of mist drifted across Howell's vision. He waved them away, his thoughts in turmoil. Thousands of enchantments from Waxing Gibbous sent through the mirror to feed Lord Skinner's hunger. Mr Bones must know. Yes, of course Mr Bones knew, and so he wanted to change the covenant.

The smell of magic grew stronger, like something long dead. Lord Skinner and Mr Bones were at war, Howell thought helplessly, and he and Ava were stuck in the middle of it.

Lord Skinner's gaze hovered somewhere between Howell and Ava. 'When your parents died, Miss Harcourt,' he said, 'I took the opportunity to bring you back to Wyse. I didn't know what your connection with the Unworld would do, but, I hoped, after the magic your father used . . .' He tailed off, struggling for words. 'Well,' he said, 'one must always hope. I'm glad you are here. Now we can fight Mr Bones together.'

Ava's shoulders slumped.

She was going to agree, Howell thought.

He shook her. 'Ava, don't listen.'

'You don't want me around you,' she said dully. 'I've caused enough trouble. Mr Bones has got Matthew. What else can we do?'

'You can run,' Lunette said. Her voice sounded strange. She pointed at the open back door.

Howell turned to look, and a cry rose in his chest. Something moved in the darkness outside: a long, thin shape with limbs that swung in odd, jerky motions, and every time the thing moved he heard it rattle.

CHAPTER 27

A skeleton is stalking you. Do you . . .

    (a) run,

    (b) order the skeleton to stop,

    (c) hide, or

    (d) do something else?

The correct answer is (e): do whatever you like: nothing will help. But I thought you might like a little quiz to pass the time while waiting for the inevitable.

The Book

The skeleton stepped over the kitchen threshold and paused, turning from side to side to look at them all. Howell's chest ached as if his heart had stopped beating.

'No!' Lord Skinner gasped, staggering back. 'He can't do this.'

The skeleton flexed its fingers.

If Mr Bones sent a skeleton after you, it didn't matter where you ran – it would hunt you down. Strangely, Howell felt almost relieved. Now he didn't have to keep constantly worrying, waiting for the rattle of bones.

Lunette thrust something into Howell's hand. He looked down and saw The Book.

'Run,' she said. 'The Book has told you where.'

She threw a hat at the skeleton. It exploded into a rainbow shower of bright light, filling the kitchen with a multicoloured blur.

'You're the guardians,' Lunette said. 'Both of you. Go – you can do it.'

The colours started to clear from the air. The skeleton lunged at them. Lunette grabbed a pan from the table and swung it.

Howell dragged Ava back out of the way. He caught a glimpse of the skeleton's dark outline reaching out, and Lunette clinging on to it, then he reached the door to the banqueting hall and kicked it shut behind him.

Ava wrenched her arm free. 'What are you doing?'

'It doesn't want Lunette. It wants The Book – it wants us. It'll come after us.'

As if to confirm his words, something thumped on the door, forcing it open a crack. Howell heard Lord Skinner shouting. 'Get out of my house! Take her and go!' Then a louder thump and Lord Skinner yelling in pain. Howell hoped Lunette had hit him.

He ran through the banqueting hall towards the gleaming mirrors in the entrance hall, pulling Ava behind him. Another crash from the kitchen. He winced.

Ava overtook him at the door. The mirrors waited. Two long rows of doors into the Unworld, all of them locked. Howell's palms prickled with sweat. Reflected in the nearest glass, he saw the skeleton burst through the door into the banqueting hall. It paused, shaking away bits of broken wood. Then it turned slowly from side to side and started across the room towards them. It wasn't in any hurry – why should it be when they were trapped?

Ava pressed her hands against the nearest mirror. Howell joined her, willing the glass to change but, as before, it remained flat and cold.

'Come on,' Howell breathed.

The skeleton was almost at the door. Lunette raced out of the kitchen and threw a saucepan at it. It batted the pan aside and kept coming. Howell tried to tear his gaze off the reflection in the glass, but he couldn't.

Ava gripped his hand painfully tight. 'This isn't working.'

It had to work. Think! What had he been doing when he'd opened mirror seventy-seven? He'd been cleaning it. And . . . and thinking about how he had no magic, and it was like a big emptiness inside him.

Howell didn't feel empty any more.

The skeleton stepped into the entrance hall. And the mirror turned misty. The reflection of the room and the skeleton bulged, distorted and disappeared. Howell heard the click of bones but he didn't turn round – he didn't dare.

Lunette shouted something, but her voice seemed far away and he couldn't make out what she'd said. The weight of The Book dragged him into the mist.

Howell felt his hand separate from Ava's.

'Ava,' he said, remembering in time. 'Come through.'

He stepped forward and the world turned silver.

And then he was stepping out of the mirror. A sheet caught around his face and he couldn't see a thing, but he felt the pressure of Ava's hand again, squeezed it reassuringly and pushed the sheet aside.

'Hello, Will,' he said.

Will leaped up from Master Tudur's chair with a scream of fright. Howell almost laughed at the sight of him, but then he saw the state of the gallery and he gasped in alarm. At least half the mirrors were uncovered, the dust sheets thrown in heaps on the floor. And the mist. It flowed in shimmering strands, filling the floor and heaping up over the one mirror that still stood covered. Mirror seventy-seven, Howell supposed.

'What's happened here?' he asked. 'Where's Master Tudur?'

Will spluttered and stammered, trying to get words out. 'You've brought a human through. How? That mirror shouldn't be working.'

Howell let go of Ava's hand. 'It is now. Will, please calm down. I can explain.'

'Explain what? Mr Bones is looking for you. He said you're an anti-humanist, and the station guards are patrolling the streets looking for traitors. They've taken Master Tudur to Waxing Gibbous. Mr Bones left me here to keep watch.'

In case anyone came through a mirror here, Howell thought. It was strange – either he'd grown taller in the past few days or Will had shrunk.

'I'm not an anti-humanist,' he said. 'Mr Bones lied to you. I think he's been lying to everyone. Ava is my friend.'

'Your friend?' Ava and Will both echoed, Ava with a worried frown and Will with a look of horror.

Howell nodded firmly. 'My friend. That's mirror seventy-seven, isn't it?' he asked, nodding at the covered shape surrounded by mist. 'It's letting magic into the human world. We need to smash it.'

'Mr Bones said not to touch it,' Will said. The whining note in his voice was starting to annoy Howell.

'You're a coward,' Howell said. 'I bet you didn't even try to help Master Tudur, did you? You only thought about saving yourself.'

Will's eyes flashed with rage. 'I'm not a coward.'

'Prove it. Disobey Mr Bones. Break the mirror.'

Will swung at him.

The blow connected and Howell's vision turned bright with specks of light. He struck back without thinking.

'Stop!' Ava snapped. Her voice shocked them both into silence.

Will stepped back, his face flushed and angry. 'You can't tell me what to do.'

'Actually, I can,' Ava said. 'I'm human – that means I can order you to do anything and you have to obey.'

Will clenched his fists. 'Not on this side of the mirror.' But Howell saw doubt in his eyes.

'Do you want to try it?' Ava asked. 'Shall I order you to stand on your head or take off all your clothes?' Her gaze hardened. 'Or shall I make you do something more dangerous, like telling Mr Bones that you are a traitor and he should lock you up in Waxing Gibbous?'

She looked small and ordinary in her grey dress with smudges of dirt on her hands and face, but the look in her eyes was as hard as iron. Howell would have hugged her if he'd dared, but she seemed more in a mood for hitting people than hugging them.

Will's shoulders slumped. 'I'm just following orders. It's not my fault.'

That was what Luel had said – just following orders.

Howell walked to the door. 'We're leaving, and you'd better not tell anyone you saw us or Ava will come back for you. You can tidy the gallery up too.'

He opened the door and looked out. Mist swirled in familiar patterns, smelling of roses and old tea. Home. Howell was quite surprised to find he'd missed it.

CHAPTER 28

58 Victoria Road, Wyse. Mist coils in through a broken window and settles over a table where supper is spread. The family come in and find that the tablecloth has turned into a snake and is swallowing the sandwiches.

And at the theatre . . . No, you don't want to know what's going to happen at the theatre. But it involves carnivorous seats and lots of screaming.

The Book

Charles sat in the empty bedroom, his case notes spread out around him. *Mr Bones*, he wrote, underlining it twice, and then *Lord Skinner*. Empty cups lay on the floor – he'd drunk all the milk; it seemed a shame to waste it. His sisters had long since gone to bed and he'd heard his parents come up the stairs about an hour ago. Charles still couldn't sleep. He wished he'd argued more with Ava and Howell. He should have insisted on going with them.

Lord Skinner wants Ava and Howell to open the mirrors. Why? To give himself more power over

Wyse? And why was Ava behaving so strangely?
What secret is she hiding?

Too many questions and no answers. He was supposed to be investigating, not sitting here scribbling notes.

The church clock struck eleven. Lord Skinner would have returned to Waning Crescent hours ago, wondering where Ava and Howell were, no doubt.

Mrs Footer started to howl.

This was no good, Charles thought. He couldn't sit and do nothing. Anything could be happening at Waning Crescent.

He put down his papers and crept on to the landing, past his sisters' room to his parents' bedroom door.

He always hated owning up to things he'd done because his mother always looked so disappointed. Tonight, however, neither parent wasted time scolding him once he'd explained.

They got up quickly, reaching for their clothes.

'You should have come to us straight away,' his father said. 'If you'd told us earlier, I could have gone to Constable Blackson for help.'

'Constable Blackson can't help,' Charles said. 'He doesn't know anything about the Unworld. We're not dealing with normal people. This is fairy magic – proper fairy magic, not the stuff put on for tourists.'

'And how do you propose fighting magic?' His mother heaved a sigh. 'No, don't even think about that – I don't want you fighting magic at all. You stay here with your sisters. Your father and I will round up Freedom for Fair Folk and we'll fetch Constable Blackson. Then we'll go to Waning Crescent and see what Lord Skinner has to say for himself.' She paused, buttoning up her shoes, and her gaze drifted away from Charles. 'I'm sure there's just been a misunderstanding. Lord Skinner is a fine gentleman. He'll sort it all out.'

They only had to say his name to start thinking he was wonderful.

Charles pulled his mother round to face him. 'Listen to yourself. It's like he's put an enchantment on everyone to make us all like him. Do you like him, really?'

His mother started to push him away, but then stopped. 'I don't know. I suppose . . .'

'Lord Skinner's always done his best for us,' Charles's father said, but he didn't look entirely certain now either. 'You go to bed, Charles. I'm sure everything will be fine, but we'll be safe enough going in a crowd together.'

He'd started them wondering: that was the best he could do for now. Charles went back to his room and waited. Soon he heard voices, and then the front door opened and closed.

His parents had told him to go back to bed, but they hadn't made him promise. He wouldn't be breaking his word if he disobeyed.

Charles buttoned up his jacket. 'Do you want to come out?' he asked Mrs Footer.

To his surprise, the dog jumped up.

Outside, mist coated everything, blurring all the houses into the same dark mass. The air smelled of smoke and roses and damp earth. A single street lamp outside the church struggled against the gloom. Charles's clothes stuck damply to him as he walked. He held a hand up in front of his face and waggled his fingers. He could barely see them. He could walk right past someone in this and they'd never know he was there.

Carriages blocked the main street: holidaymakers deciding they couldn't spend one more night in this place.

'This is why we don't have magic in England,' one woman complained loudly as Charles passed. 'We never get this sort of trouble in Bath.'

Her voice was swallowed up by screaming as people streamed out of the theatre. A lot of the ladies' skirts were in tatters, and the men's trousers too. Charles stopped to stare as one man ran right by him, wearing a top hat and evening jacket and only a few rags left below his waist.

'My chair just tried to eat me,' the man shouted. He plunged on into the mist.

Charles bent to pick up a fallen advertising board.

Mr Radcot, gentleman conjuror. All wishes guaranteed.
Mr Edmund Footer, conjuror by royal appointment to Queen Victoria. Private audiences granted Monday–Friday.
Langhile and Gaddesby, conjurors.
Children's parties a speciality (ask about our summer offers).

Conjurors could summon the Fair Folk into mirrors and command them to do anything, Charles thought. *How do you propose fighting magic?* Mum had asked. That was easy: with more magic.

Mr Bones was one of the Fair Folk. That meant he could be summoned into a mirror, and if he could be summoned, he could be commanded.

Charles glanced down at Mrs Footer. The little dog shook herself and twitched her shoulders as if she was trying to shrug.

It was worth a try, Charles decided. Instead of continuing to Waning Crescent, he turned and hurried off in the direction of the Footers' home.

Howell clutched The Book in both arms and led Ava through the narrow lanes of Unwyse. Mist swirled around them, forming faces and strange animals and long strands that looked like branches about to burst into flower. The moon was only just visible right overhead: an almost perfect circle of silver light.

After Ava's outburst at Will she'd been quiet, and she barely looked at Howell as they walked. Howell remembered how sick he'd felt the first morning he'd woken up in Wyse and it had hit him that he was in a different world. He unwound an arm from The Book and offered Ava his hand.

'It'll be fine,' he said. 'Lunette wouldn't send us to Madame Brille if it wasn't safe.' He quite enjoyed the feeling of being in charge for a change.

Footsteps crunched in the mist behind. Howell pulled Ava back against the wall as a voice rang out.

'What are you two doing?'

Guards.

Howell couldn't see, but he was sure if the mist cleared he'd see red uniforms. He stood rigid.

'You should be at home. Don't you know there's a curfew?'

And another voice answered. 'We're on our way, aren't we? We've just finished work.'

Howell let all his breath out in a rush. The guards hadn't seen him and Ava. They'd stopped someone else on the street, just by the end of the lane.

The conversation continued. The guards wanted to search the people they'd stopped, and the people complained and finally gave in.

'You can go,' one of the guards said at last. 'Hurry on home.'

A few more muffled words, and the footsteps moved away.

Howell waited until silence returned, then he shifted his feet cautiously. He could make out the dark shape of the guards in the mist, turning away.

'I think it's safe now,' Ava whispered.

A guard stopped, turned and took a step towards the lane. 'Who's there?'

Howell clenched his fists.

Ava stepped away from him out into the lane. Howell caught at her. 'What are you doing?'

'You should run,' she said, her voice tight and frightened. 'I've caused you enough trouble. Mr Bones already has Matthew, so I don't mind if I'm caught.'

'I mind,' Howell said. He rooted about in the rubbish for a stone and threw it in the direction of the guards. Then he grabbed Ava's hand and ran. The guards shouted and gave chase.

Howell's heart pounded. Ava tripped and he nearly lost his grip on her. He imagined more guards coming, threading through the lanes to cut off their escape.

Then another stone sailed over Howell's head and bounced off the wall. A guard shouted behind them.

More stones flew. Howell ducked down low, trying to see what was happening. Figures ran through the mist. A boy appeared beside Howell – one of the group who'd attacked him the night he met Lunette.

Howell groaned. 'Can you beat me up later? I'm a bit busy.'

'You're in luck,' the boy said. 'We're not with the anti-humanists today. Madame Brille said to hurry.'

He raced at the guards, then at the last moment swerved down a side alley. Other boys joined him, jeering and throwing stones. The guards ran after them, and in a moment the lane was empty.

'Who was that?' Ava whispered.

Howell pressed his back against the wall, trying to stop himself shaking. 'Someone I met once. I think we're nearly there.'

They walked on, Ava feeling her way with one hand on the wall.

Howell's stomach churned, and not just from the close escape. Mad Madame Brille, he thought, who turned people into earwigs. He'd spent his life avoiding the road where she lived and now he was hurrying along it.

And there it was – a narrow door with the number 77 glowing in the mist. Howell wiped his palms on his trousers and raised his hand to knock.

The door flew open and a pair of thin arms hauled them both inside.

CHAPTER 29

Lord Skinner backs away, one hand to his mouth. The skeleton ignores him and walks back through the banqueting hall to pick up Lunette. She dangles from the bone shoulder. Slowly the skeleton climbs the stairs to the door that stands open at the top.

Sometime later, Lord Skinner will check the room and find it empty.

The Book

It took a full minute of knocking on Mr Footer's door before the conjuror opened it: Charles timed it. The conjuror looked as if he hadn't slept – or washed, or shaved – in a week. His moustache bristled as if it was trying to escape from his face, and his eyes looked red and bloodshot.

'You're the Brunels' boy,' he said, peering at Charles in exhausted bewilderment. 'What do you want?'

Charles took a deep breath. 'I know you won't believe me, but this dog really is your mother. She got accidentally enchanted.'

Mr Footer rubbed his eyes, not really seeming to see the dog or Charles properly. 'There's no enchantment on the animal,' he said. 'I don't know what joke you think you're playing, but this is not funny. Now go home or I'll tell your mother you were bothering me.'

Charles didn't move. He hadn't expected Mr Footer to believe him, but an investigator doesn't give up after their first try.

'I can prove it,' he said. 'I just need you to conjure a fairy for me.'

'You need me to do *what*?' Mr Footer's moustache jumped. 'My mother is missing, the whole town is going mad and you come here talking about dogs and conjuring. Go home.'

'I'm sorry, but I can't.' *A good policeman is always polite, always persistent.* Charles took out his notebook. 'My friends and I have been collecting clues. Lord Skinner is not all he seems to be. We know he was using you to send secret orders to Unwyse. The townspeople are already on their way to Waning Crescent to demand answers, but I thought it might be faster if you used your mirror.'

He put on his most earnest expression.

Mr Footer dropped his gaze and sighed. 'Maybe you're only trying to help, but it's no use. Lord Skinner called a meeting of all the conjurors today and he confiscated our mirrors – for investigation, he said. None of us can conjure anything.' He ran his hand over his face. 'I don't know what my mother would say about this if she were here.'

It occurred to Charles that he'd rarely seen Mr Footer without his mother. Mrs Footer was always fussing around him, answering questions before he could speak, telling him what to do. Mr Footer must be quite lost without her. Charles felt a moment's sympathy for him. Mrs Footer growled and tried to bite the conjuror's ankle.

'Sorry,' Charles said, moving her away. He skimmed through his notes for the next question. 'How long have you been sending messages to Unwyse for Lord Skinner?'

Mr Footer drew himself up proudly. 'My work is confidential. I'm not at liberty to discuss it. Lord Skinner is a fine gentleman.'

Why did people have to ignore what was right in front of them? Charles wondered. But if Mr Footer wouldn't believe the evidence, Charles would have to find another way to persuade him.

'Yes, he is,' he agreed. 'And he's responsible for all the conjurors, isn't he? He must be an expert on magic.'

'Not really.' Mr Footer still scowled, but he appeared a little less sure of himself. 'I don't believe Lord Skinner knows very much about fairy magic. Certainly not as much as I do.'

'Then it would be a good idea to help him find out

what's going on here,' Charles said. 'After all, you're the expert, not him. That's why he asked you to send orders to Unwyse, because he knows you're the best conjuror in Wyse.'

Everyone had a weak point, Charles's books on investigation said, and Charles had just found Mr Footer's: his vanity. The conjuror's chest puffed up even more. 'That's true. I don't know why he didn't come to me.'

'Some of the other conjurors are on their way to Waning Crescent now,' Charles said.

They might be – his parents would be rounding up half the town to visit Lord Skinner, after all. He watched Mr Footer's expression change. He knew exactly what the conjuror was thinking: if other conjurors were going to Waning Crescent, he should go too. Otherwise, they might solve the crisis and get all the credit for it.

'Or do you think there are enough conjurors involved already?' Charles said. 'I think I heard Mr Langhile say he could handle this on his own.'

It was the last prod Mr Footer needed.

'Mr Langhile is a bumbling fool,' he growled. 'Wait there, boy. I'll get my coat.'

CHAPTER 30

The last mirrors are dying. My magic is dying. What is written must come to pass. I don't feel well. Can books get sick? If so, I think I'm coming down with something. If anyone can help, please make your way to Unwyse through the nearest working mirror. This is an emergency.

The Book

Howell had only ever seen Madame Brille from a distance before – usually when he was running away from her. Close-up, he thought he had never seen anyone so old before, or so ugly. Three pairs of spectacles wobbled on a nose that was huge and almost perfectly round, and a pair of dark eyes glinted at him through the layers of glass.

He stood uncertainly, clutching The Book and rubbing his arm where the old woman's hand had bruised him. 'Are you Madame Brille?'

'Who were you expecting?' Her face was as round as her nose, crinkly with deep wrinkles. Her hair, pure white, was pulled up into a lumpy bun on the top of her head and two more pairs of spectacles – one bright red, one yellow – peeped out. 'Take a good look,' she said. 'We have plenty of time. It's not as if Mr Bones is hunting you or anything.' She stank of lavender, even her breath.

Howell's face filled up with heat. 'Sorry. I'm Howell and this is Ava. And this . . .'

'. . . is The Book, I know.' She took off one of the pairs of glasses and replaced it with the red pair from her hair. 'The moment my niece turned up saying she needed an enchantment, I knew it would lead to trouble, and I wasn't even wearing my trouble-predicting glasses. You'd better come up.'

She started to stamp up the stairs.

'Trouble-predicting glasses?' Ava mouthed to Howell. 'What if this is a trap?'

'I heard that,' Madame Brille shouted.

Howell gave a nervous grin. 'I think we'll be safe.' Lunette had told them to come here. And, besides, after spending time in Wyse seeing people covered up with cheap enchantments, he got the feeling that Madame Brille was the opposite of all that. She was exactly what she appeared to be.

Upstairs, a fire crackled in the grate and bowls of dried flower heads stood on every surface. A table held a tea tray with a pot and three cups and saucers. It appeared that Madame Brille had been expecting them. Howell gave Ava what he hoped was a reassuring look and pushed her on into the room.

'Come in and try not to get muck on the carpets,' Madame Brille said. 'I'll just find my glasses.'

She opened a wooden box on the table and rummaged about inside. Howell saw that it contained spectacles – hundreds of them, all lined up in rows. 'What are they for?' he asked.

'Reading glasses, distance glasses, glasses for seeing friends, glasses for seeing customers, glasses for seeing when somebody's lying. Glasses for spells, glasses for enchantments, glasses for cooking, glasses for eating. Don't laugh. You'll be sorry when you're old and need glasses.'

She tried on several pairs before settling on a set with plain brown rims. 'Not what you expected an Unworld house to look like?' she asked Ava, who was staring wide-eyed. 'I bet you imagined our armchairs walked and our teapots sang to amuse us.'

Ava turned pink. 'No I didn't.'

'No,' Madame Brille said, changing glasses again and peering at her, 'maybe you didn't. There's more to you than meets the eyes, isn't there? Even my eyes. You can sit down if you like: the chairs won't eat you.'

Ava cast Howell a confused glance and they both sat down. Madame Brille began rummaging through her box of spectacles. 'Glasses for meeting new people,' she muttered, pulling out a pair with orange heart-shaped frames. 'No – wait, I need glasses for questioning visitors. Blue hearts.' She swapped them over and sat down, her eyes suddenly sharp and bright. 'How did my truth-showing enchantment work?'

Howell wasn't sure what to say. 'It . . . um . . . worked.'

'Good. I told my niece: I don't give refunds.' Madame Brille reached for the teapot and poured a bright stream of pink tea into cups. 'Euphorbia leaf – eyebright. It's quite safe to drink – might even do you some good. Now –' she settled into a low armchair – 'you'd better tell me everything.'

They took turns to talk while Madame Brille sat, lifting her various pairs of glasses up and down and occasionally stopping their story to change a pair.

'You're in quite a lot of trouble, aren't you?' she said when they'd finished. She jabbed a finger at The Book. 'You too.'

Don't blame me. I only foretell the future – I don't create it.

A lump formed in Howell's throat. 'What's going to happen to Matthew and Lunette?'

'As I don't own a magic book of prophecy,' Madame Brille said with a pointed glare at The Book, 'I have no idea.'

You'll find them in Waxing Gibbous, obviously. Mr Bones has them. Where else did you think they'd be?

Howell's stomach turned over. 'It could be worse,' he said. At least they knew now. And Waxing Gibbous was always so busy with people, that they might be able to sneak in unnoticed.

'More tea,' Madame Brille said. 'You two carry on talking. I'll be back in a minute.' She bustled out of the room.

Howell swallowed the last mouthful in his cup. It was almost cold and the bitter aftertaste made him cough.

Howell is afraid, wrote The Book. *And now Howell wishes he could throw me out of the nearest window and forget about me.*

Howell realized he was gripping the edge of The Book hard enough to leave dents in it. He unclenched his fingers.

'Yes, Book, I'm afraid,' he said. He looked up at Ava. 'I've been afraid since this all started. I wish I wasn't, but I can't help it, so I'm just going to have to carry on and do everything while I'm afraid, because if I wait until I feel braver it'll be too late.'

He fell silent.

Ava let out a long breath. 'I'm afraid too,' she said quietly.

They sat and looked at each other for a moment. At least he wasn't on his own in this, Howell thought. It made the knot in his stomach untie. He pushed The Book off his lap and sat back. 'Do you think we're really connected somehow?'

Ava looked down and started to shake her head, but then she stopped and gazed straight back at him. 'I'm sorry.'

The apology was so unexpected, Howell's mouth fell open. 'Sorry? What for?'

'I think I did something.' She pulled at her skirt. 'Something terrible. Magic was taken from a boy. You remember the letter I found on Mr Footer's desk? And Lord Skinner said I'm alive because of magic. It's true. I was very ill when I was little and I should have died, but I suddenly recovered. And then my father sold everything and moved away from Wyse. My father, who used to be a conjuror.'

'Your father was a conjuror?' Howell asked.

She nodded. 'But everyone knows fairy magic is only illusion and can't really change things.'

'*Some* fairy magic,' Madame Brille corrected, bustling back into the room with another tea tray. 'The truth-showing enchantment, for example, I put a bit of myself into that, just a few strands of hair to give it a boost. And then there's the magic inherent in all of us. If that magic is taken, it can change reality forever.'

Howell sat quite still. She was talking about him, he knew, but his mind rebelled against it. It was as if he knew but didn't want to know.

'Unwyse is the most magic-infested town in the

whole Unworld,' Madame Brille said. 'Don't you think it's odd that you'd grow up here and be the only person without magic?'

'But I'm not the only one,' Howell protested.

'Aren't you? How many people do you know who have no magic at all? Ten years ago, magic was taken from a two-year-old Unworld boy. Ten years ago, a two-year-old girl in Wyse miraculously recovered. I know, because I helped make the enchantment myself. I took your magic, Howell, and I gave it to Ava's father.'

The room felt as if it was spinning. This was the secret Ava had been hiding from him. In a way, it was worse than all Lord Skinner's secrets. Lord Skinner had stolen magic from the mirrors to keep himself alive. Ava's father had stolen it from Howell.

'You can blame me,' Madame Brille said. 'I'm the one who did it, not Ava.'

Howell nodded. He ought to feel angry, but he didn't. He wondered why that was. His magic – all of it – taken and given away. It felt as if someone was banging a drum inside his head, too loud for him to think.

Then he realized the sound was coming from downstairs. Somebody was banging on the door.

CHAPTER 31

It's getting worse. Or possibly better. Or possibly later. In any case, it's probably time to start screaming for help now.

The Book

Charles hurried through the thickening mist with Mr Footer at his side while Mrs Footer trotted ahead, tugging on her lead as if she was eager to get this over with.

'This is a complete waste of time,' Mr Footer muttered to himself. 'Lord Skinner is a fine gentleman. I'm sure there's an explanation for this.'

People didn't like to think they'd been taken in by lies, Charles thought, especially the lies of someone who was rich and respected, like Lord Skinner. Mr Footer wasn't the only one who'd been taken in, though – and Charles wasn't the only one who wanted answers. As they reached Waning Crescent, Charles saw figures through the mist.

Around twenty people were crowded together at Lord Skinner's front steps. The mist was too heavy for him to recognize them at first, but as Charles drew nearer he saw his parents, along with Reverend Stowe and all the other members of Freedom for Fair Folk. Reverend Stowe held a placard on a stick, which he waved in a vaguely embarrassed fashion.

Other townspeople had joined the group and were watching with interest. Charles spotted Constable Blackson wearing his policeman's uniform, and two of the other Wyse conjurors, as well – Mr Langhile and Mr Gaddesby.

A flurry of mist lifted Charles's cap off his head and whisked it away. 'Hey!' he shouted. Several people turned.

'Charles!' his mother said. 'I told you to stay at home.'

'I know. I'm sorry.' He chased after his cap and retrieved it. 'I've brought Mr Footer. And . . .' He almost said 'Mrs Footer' and caught himself. 'And the dog,' he added.

'Go home to your sisters, Charles,' his father said sternly.

Charles stared at him innocently. 'What? In this weather, at this time of night, all by myself?'

A carriage dashed by. Quite an ordinary-looking one, except that it was barely twelve inches tall and it was drawn by a team of blue-furred mice. Mrs Footer pounced at it, but it disappeared along the crescent. Several ladies shrieked as it passed.

Mr Footer shook his coat back. 'This is too much. Where is Lord Skinner? Taking our mirrors, letting magic infect our town. It's time he did something about it.'

The conjurors, Mr Langhile and Mr Gaddesby, muttered agreement. Reverend Stowe brandished his placard. 'What do we want? Answers! When do we want them?'

'Soon, if you please!' someone shouted back.

Charles waited. His parents gazed at him, then his father sighed and shook his head. 'Just stay out of trouble.'

Charles grinned and joined the back of the crowd. Pity he didn't have a placard to wave, but Reverend Stowe's was the only one. The whole group stood politely, everyone looking at everyone else and nobody making a move towards Lord Skinner's front doors and the bell pull.

'I don't think he's there,' Mr Footer said uncertainly.

'Of course he is.' Lord Skinner wouldn't still be waiting in the churchyard. But if he was home, he must have noticed them all outside. Why hadn't he opened the door already?

Mrs Footer nipped Charles's ankle. He looked down at her. 'You think I should . . . ?' He didn't want to be the one to ring the bell.

Mrs Footer growled, and then, surprisingly, she nodded and tugged on her lead.

'Charles, what are you doing?' his mother asked as he squeezed through the crowd. He grasped the bell rope and pulled it. The bell clanged harshly, echoing across the crescent. Charles held his breath.

Nothing happened. But now that Charles had made the first move, others joined in.

Mr Footer reached across his shoulder and rang the bell again. 'Skinner, we know you're in there. Open the doors.'

Charles scrambled over the railing and peered through a window. 'I can see lights inside.' He climbed back, took the bell pull and tugged it, ringing the bell again and again until the noised echoed all the way along the crescent. 'We won't go until you come out,' he shouted. 'We'll break the windows to get in if we have to.'

'Charles!' Mrs Brunel scolded.

'He doesn't know we don't mean it,' Charles said. He reached over the railing and banged on the nearest window.

'Freedom for Fair Folk!' Reverend Stowe shouted, and began knocking the door enthusiastically with his placard. A few other people joined in, shouting and banging on the door and windows.

And then, at last, the door flew open.

Everyone fell silent. Reverend Stowe tried to hide his placard behind his back.

Charles was used to the sight of Lord Skinner

dressed as a lord – expensive suits and tall silk hats, polished boots. He was not used to the sight of Lord Skinner in a vast gold dressing gown and red slippers, his hair flattened over his scalp, not quite covering the folds of skin beneath.

'Yes?' Lord Skinner said. 'Can I help you?' The hand he rested on the door frame didn't seem to belong to him – it was far too thin and covered in brown age spots.

People shuffled back.

'We want to know what's going on,' Charles's father said. 'Um, that is, if you don't mind.'

Lord Skinner tucked his dressing gown tighter around his bulk. 'As you can see, I have retired for the night. Maybe you'd care to leave a card and we can arrange a time for you to continue this little protest tomorrow.'

Protesters didn't leave calling cards, Charles thought. Around him people shuffled their feet and some of them started to edge back down the steps. They were still under Lord Skinner's spell, doing everything he said.

Mrs Footer flattened herself to the ground and growled. A patch of mist drifted by and Charles found himself looking at Lord Skinner through it. He gaped. For a second he saw Lord Skinner's face drooping in grey-blue folds from his eyes to his chin, as if there was no flesh underneath but just air slowly escaping.

His faded blue eyes appeared bloodshot and his gaze never rested but darted back and forth, as if afraid of what he might see.

'What have you done with Ava and Howell?' Charles asked loudly.

The mist cleared around Lord Skinner and he looked more like himself again. 'Howell? I don't know anyone called Howell.' He gripped the door frame harder. 'As for the Harcourts, I haven't seen either of them since this morning. I expect they've run away. The Harcourts always were a strange family.'

'That's true,' Mr Langhile agreed.

Charles noticed a slight shimmer to the mist and smelled burning. 'It's not true at all. You're just believing it because Lord Skinner says so. He's enchanting us – he's been doing it all along.' It was so obvious now that he couldn't understand why everyone else didn't see it.

Charles turned to Mr Footer, who was watching strands of mist coil into dog shapes. 'You wanted to ask Lord Skinner about your mirror, remember?'

Mr Footer jumped out of his reverie. 'So I did.' He rubbed his eyes and blinked several times. 'Well, what about it, Lord Skinner? That mirror was my property, purchased fair and square, and you had no right to take it. What are these investigations you're doing with it, anyway?'

'The investigations are a matter of government

security,' Lord Skinner snapped back. 'I'm not at liberty to discuss them. I have already told you that, you should stay in your homes until this situation is resolved. I am far too busy to talk right now.'

'Busy?' Charles said. 'Didn't you say you were in bed?'

Mrs Footer snarled agreement.

Lord Skinner started to close the doors, but Mr Footer put his hand against one. 'We're not going until we have answers.'

'When exactly will we be permitted to leave our homes?' Reverend Stowe asked. 'I had to cancel all my visits today, and the mist is getting worse, not better.'

Charles doubted that anyone had ever spoken back to Lord Skinner before. Other people were murmuring now, as well.

'I don't believe you're a fine gentleman at all,' Mr Footer said suddenly. His voice and his eyebrows rose in matching surprise at his own daring. 'What's your game, Skinner?'

Lord Skinner deflated even more. Whatever confidence he'd managed to summon was draining out of him and, with it, his control over the situation.

Mrs Footer broke free from her lead and darted between Lord Skinner's legs into Waning Crescent. Charles made a grab for her and missed.

Then, before Lord Skinner could stop it, before Charles himself realized what was happening, the whole group was pushing through the doors, placard and all.

Lord Skinner put out his arms. 'Stop!'

They ignored him. The people at the front shoved him backwards and so many other people were crowding behind that they all kept going, pushing and shoving past Charles, until they were all inside Waning Crescent and he was standing alone on the doorstep. He took out his notebook – a good policeman should always be ready to record evidence – and followed them inside.

CHAPTER 32

*The factory of Waxing Gibbous is old. As old as bones.
Although, as a single year spent within its walls feels like
seven, it's hard to keep track of time once you're in there.*

The Book

Another knock. Heavier this time and repeating until the thudding seemed to go right through to Ava's bones. She supposed they ought to do something but her mind was a blank space. All she could think about was the awful truth: she'd taken all of Howell's magic, spoiled his life. She should have died of measles, then Howell would still have magic and Matthew would be free to do whatever he wanted without having to worry about her.

Bang!

Madame Brille got to her feet and pulled a bag out from under a cushion. 'That will keep The Book safe,' she said, giving it to Howell, or rather, dropping it in his lap because he still sat as if turned to stone.

'Is it enchanted?' Ava asked.

'No – just a bag.' She took two pairs of wire-rimmed spectacles out of the box. 'These are my mind-your-own-business glasses. They won't quite make you invisible but they'll stop people from noticing you. I had to make them in a hurry and they won't last long, but they'll get you to Waxing Gibbous.'

A voice shouted downstairs. 'Open this door!'

Ava hooked the glasses over her ears with trembling fingers. The flimsy wire felt as if it would break at any minute. She'd expected the room to look different through the lenses, but everything was exactly the same: the fire in the grate, Madame Brille, Howell looking at her with wide eyes.

Howell put his glasses on. 'I can still see Ava.'

'That's because Ava *is* your business. Don't worry.' She crossed the room and threw open the window. 'Go away!' she cried out. 'I'm a harmless old widow and I was fast asleep.'

She didn't look harmless. She looked as if she was considering dropping something heavy out of the window. Ava edged closer to Howell.

'I'm sorry.'

'Stop apologizing. It wasn't your fault.'

'Mr Bones says you are harbouring traitors,' one of the guards shouted up. 'Open this door or we'll break it down.'

Madame Brille heaved a sigh. 'Give me a moment.' She slammed the window shut and turned back to

Ava and Howell. 'Stay behind me,' she said quietly. 'When I open the door, you can slip out.'

Ava curled her fingers into her palms and blew out a breath. 'Howell, if this goes wrong, you have to leave me behind and run.' He'd already spent all his magic saving her life once; she couldn't let him be captured because of her.

Howell shook his head and started to say something, but Madame Brille cut him off. 'Get ready,' she said, and she opened the door.

Four guards rushed in. The first two seized Madame Brille and pinned her to the wall. 'You're under arrest,' one of them said. All four of them ignored Ava and Howell completely.

Madame Brille flapped her hands weakly. 'I'm a poor old grandmother. I'll come quietly – just don't go upstairs.'

The guards rushed straight up the stairs.

'Don't touch my spectacles,' Madame Brille shouted, stamping after them.

Ava turned her head and met Howell's gaze. They both stood frozen for a second, then, together, they nodded and slipped out unseen into the misty lane.

The streets were almost empty – the guards had said something about a curfew, Ava remembered – and the few people who passed by did so without even looking her way. It felt odd, almost as if she wasn't there at all.

'Let me take The Book for a while,' she said, catching up with Howell. He shrugged her away, but she took the bag from his shoulder anyway. 'Howell, I'm really sorry. If I knew how to give your magic back to you, I would.'

He finally paused and looked at her properly. She couldn't work out the expression on his face.

'Howell?'

He dropped his gaze. 'We need to rescue Matthew and Lunette,' he said. 'Everything else can wait.' He turned and pointed to a pair of long chimneys looming out of the mist a little way behind the Mirror Station. 'There. Waxing Gibbous.'

The chimney belched out a cloud of black smoke. Ava's stomach cramped as if she hadn't eaten for a week. The crescent on her cheek burned, but when she rubbed her hand over her face, her skin felt icy cold. Matthew and Lunette were trapped in there. With Mr Bones. Ava felt a shudder go through her. She pushed the bag up on her shoulder and tried to smile, though her face felt rigid.

'Come on, then.'

Close up, Waxing Gibbous appeared even worse than Ava had imagined. The featureless walls were so filthy with grime, soot and slimy green moss that it was impossible to tell what colour they'd been to start with. There were no windows, just one square door where the guards stood. Even the mist was grey here, more like smoke.

Men, women and children stood around in small groups, none of them talking. They all looked as if they were almost asleep standing up.

'Break-time,' Howell said. 'They let people out every eight hours to get some fresh air.' He grimaced. 'If you can call it fresh.'

Ava paused, trying to catch her breath. 'Why is it so ugly?'

Howell shrugged. 'Mr Bones built it. He doesn't like to waste time on making things look pretty. Anyway, when you're inside, you stop noticing.'

It sounded horrendous. 'Why don't people run away?'

'Some of them are prisoners, and Mr Bones put enchantments on them so they can't. Other people just need the work. The kids are all on apprenticeships. You have to do a year's work here to qualify for any other job in Unwyse.' He shook his head, staring at the dark walls. 'Some people enjoy the work, believe it or not. They discover magical talents they didn't know they had.'

'But you never did,' said Ava, 'because I'd already taken your magic.'

Howell frowned. 'Will you stop going on about that?'

A bell clanged. Ava looked up to see all the

people shuffling into a line.

'Come on,' Howell whispered, moving to join them. 'Keep your head down and walk slowly. Getting into Waxing Gibbous is easy – no one would ever go through the doors unless they had to, so nobody checks. Getting out again will probably be harder,' he added.

The factory doors swung back with a noise that hurt Ava's ears. She pulled her bonnet forward, suddenly aware of how out of place she would look if anyone noticed her, with her plain brown human hair. But no one paid her any attention. Madame Brille's glasses were still working, it seemed.

A guard came down the line, handing out packets of food wrapped in brown paper. Ava slipped past him, keeping The Book gripped to her side. The people in front of her, were opening their packets and stuffing food into their mouths.

'You only get two meals a day in here,' Howell said. 'Small meals. Mr Bones thinks people work better if they're a bit hungry.'

Mr Bones was the very opposite of Lord Skinner, Ava thought, remembering Matthew complaining about the heavy lunches. She summoned up a smile. 'Mr Bones is friends with skeletons. I don't think I'd listen to him about food.'

Then she took a deep breath and stepped through the doors into Waxing Gibbous.

The noise hit her like a solid thing: clanks and rattles like a hundred carriages, people shouting, great gusts of steam hissing into the air. There were vast, dark machines with bits that went up and down, constantly slamming and rebounding. One half of the factory was entirely taken up with metal tables, and the tabletops moved, squealing constantly around in impossible loops.

The air itself felt heavy here, and Ava battled to walk, feeling as if she was wading through water. Howell pulled her between long benches where people were gluing dead leaves on to sticks. Ava put her hand on one and it came away covered in glue and blue fluff. How had Howell survived a whole year in this place? She knew it was late and she hadn't slept in ages, but she felt too tired to talk, or even to think properly.

'Ava!' Howell said.

The sudden tremor in his voice cut through her tiredness. She turned to look and stifled a gasp of panic. People in red uniforms were making their way between the tables, and with them Ava saw a tall, thin man in a dark suit. People scattered out of his path as he walked.

Ava's mouth turned paper dry. She already knew who the man was, even before Howell whispered.

'Mr Bones. He's here.'

CHAPTER 33

Feeling scared yet? Try looking in a mirror and imagine all that nasty, sick worry passing from you to your reflection. Put it in the mirror and you won't feel so bad. Better now? Warning: may not work with common mirrors. Fairy enchantments are never guaranteed and results may not be as expected.

The Book

The throng of people spread out all along the hall of Waning Crescent. Charles gaped as he saw the mirrors, and he wasn't the only one. He could easily tell the people who, like him, had never been inside Waning Crescent before, because their mouths were all open.

Their reflections bounced from mirror to mirror, floor to ceiling, all the way along the grand hallway. Candlelight flickered around him – the huge chandeliers overhead were all fully lit and other candles burned in holders on the walls, filling the air with the scent of dripping wax.

Lord Skinner stood in the middle, waving his arms. 'This is my home and you are all intruding. Please leave now.'

'Not until you tell us what's going on here,' Mr Footer said. 'What is this mist? Where's my mirror? And where is my mother?' He pushed through the crowd and stood face to face with Lord Skinner.

Lord Skinner's gaze darted sideways. 'I don't know where your mother is. I'm sorry she's missing, but it's nothing to do with me.'

'You were quick enough to take over, the night she disappeared,' Mr Footer said.

Charles spotted Mrs Footer cowering under a table and he crawled underneath to pick her up. People continued arguing.

'Souvenirs coming to life, scaring away my customers . . .'

'You had no business taking our mirrors. How are we supposed to earn a living now?'

'Fair Folk are people too, you know.' That was Reverend Stowe, his voice half lost in the general noise.

Charles crawled back out from under the table and squeezed between the reverend and Constable Blackson, holding Mrs Footer up so she could watch too.

Lord Skinner tried to shepherd everyone back towards the doors. 'Please, everybody calm down. Go home.'

But nobody listened.

'There's my mirror!' Mr Gaddesby exclaimed. He ran to the far end of the hall, lifted a gilt frame off the wall and turned it over to display his name on the back. 'We'll soon find out what's happening.' He spread his hands over the glass. 'Mirror, I command you to open up the Unworld before our disbelieving eyes.'

Charles wondered how many people here had disbelieving eyes. But, disbelieving or not, the mirror remained as it was, reflecting the hall and the faces around it. Mr Gaddesby frowned and shook it.

'*Aperire spectaculum. Speculum magica*,' Mr Langhile said helpfully. Or unhelpfully, as it turned out, because nothing happened.

'What have you done to it, Skinner?' Mr Gaddesby said.

Lord Skinner thrust his chest out, but Charles noted the glint of panic in his eyes. 'I have done nothing. The mirror simply failed. It's sad, but it seems that the last of the fairy magic is disappearing.'

'Judging by the mist, the fairy magic seems to be getting stronger,' Charles said.

Lord Skinner's face filled with annoyance. 'I assure you . . .'

People muttered. A couple of ladies began opening doors along the hall and peering inside.

'Leave those rooms alone,' Lord Skinner said.

'They contain nothing interesting.'

'I've found some more mirrors,' one of the ladies said.

Everyone crowded to look.

'That one's mine,' Mr Footer said. He brought it out into the hall.

'It's just an ordinary mirror,' Lord Skinner protested. 'From Cornwall. It may happen to look like yours, but it's quite unmagical, I assure you.'

Mr Footer set it down against the wall. '*Ostende Unwysium!*'

Nothing happened for a moment or two. Maybe Lord Skinner had told the truth about the mirrors dying, after all. But then Mr Footer put his hand on the mirror and the glass blurred and turned the colour of mist.

A murmur of surprise ran through the watchers. Mr Footer straightened slowly and turned to face Lord Skinner.

'An unmagical mirror from Cornwall, is it?'

'Maybe I mixed it up with another one. You can take it away with you now. I don't need it any more.'

And then a low sound of 'Oooh!' rippled through the hall because Mr Footer's mirror cleared, but instead of showing the hall at Waning Crescent, the glass revealed a blue-haired girl. She wore a dark red jacket and sat with her head down, picking her nails and scowling with boredom.

Mr Footer coughed. 'Um, excuse me?'

The Unworld girl looked up and her scowl changed to surprise. 'This isn't your usual time. What do you want? It had better be quick. We're busy tonight.'

Having met two of the Fair Folk already, Charles thought he should be getting used to seeing them, but he still felt a shiver go through him, as if the air around had suddenly turned icy. Still holding Mrs Footer, he squeezed past his mother to the front of the group.

'We want to see Mr Bones,' he called out.

Everyone turned to stare at him, even the Unworld girl.

Lord Skinner edged away from the mirror. 'No, no, we don't want to see Mr Bones, not right now. We don't want anything. That will be all, thank you.'

A malicious smirk flickered across the girl's face. 'This isn't your mirror,' she said. 'You don't command it – he does.' She jabbed a finger at Mr Footer. 'What do you want?'

Mr Footer swallowed. 'Mr Bones,' he said. He glanced back at Charles. 'Yes, whoever or whatever he is. Be so kind as to fetch him.'

'No!' Lord Skinner shouted.

Charles jumped, not so much because of its volume, but because of the fear in Lord Skinner's voice. Charles wondered whether he'd done the right thing asking to see Mr Bones. Too late to change his mind now, though: he'd made the request and Mr Footer had repeated it. Charles kept hold of Mrs Footer and edged back. He wanted to be close to the doors in case he had to run.

The Unworld girl laughed. The sound had an edge of cold malice to it, sharper than broken glass.

Everybody stopped fidgeting and watched breathlessly. Even Mrs Footer stopped wriggling.

'You want to see Mr Bones?' the blue-haired girl said. 'That's easily done.' She jabbed a finger outward at Lord Skinner. 'Put *him* in front of the mirror.'

Lord Skinner gave a cry of terror and ran. The crowd chased him and caught him halfway to the doors. Several people – Charles's father among them, Charles noticed – took the protesting lord by the arms and began pushing him back along the hall to where Mr Footer waited with the mirror.

Lord Skinner's slippers skidded on the floor as he scrabbled his feet desperately. He'd lost control of everyone. Whatever magic he'd been using to make people like him appeared to have broken. Charles didn't know whether to be glad or to feel sorry for him.

The crowd came to a halt in front of the mirror and turned Lord Skinner round to face it. He seemed to deflate a little, as if he'd realized there was no point fighting any longer. His reflection, which had been distorted before, now grew thinner and longer.

And then thinner and longer again.

Mrs Footer growled softly. Several people

exclaimed, in surprise or fear, or just because everyone else was doing it.

Charles blinked. In the glass, instead of Lord Skinner's reflection, he saw a tall, thin man with dark hair, a long, sharp nose and a face that seemed to be made entirely of straight lines.

The people surrounding Lord Skinner drew back, leaving him in the middle of a bare circle of floor.

'Who – what – are you?' Mr Footer stammered.

The skeletal man looked at him. His eyes were dark and deep, seeming more like holes than eyes.

Mr Footer made a small whimpering noise and took another step back.

'I am Mr Bones,' the apparition said. 'I am this man's reflection, brought to life by magic and filled with malice. Why have you summoned me?'

CHAPTER 34

You're probably wondering how that blue-haired mirror-operator knew Mr Bones's secret. You were? Well done. I like an observant reader. The blue-haired girl is observant, too, especially when it comes to Mr Bones. She'll make a good police officer one day.

The Book

Mr Bones: here. Howell dug his fingers into Ava's arm. His thoughts were so muddy that all he could do was stand and stare in dismay.

And then Mr Bones disappeared.

Howell blinked. One moment there he was, striding across the factory floor, the next he was gone, leaving only a pale patch of mist and a group of guards who paused and gazed at each other in confusion.

The bridge of Howell's nose tingled. His vision went wonky for a moment, then cleared, and when he looked at Ava he saw that Madame Brille's glasses had vanished. He put a hand to his own face and felt the empty space.

'A human!' someone shouted.

Howell groaned. *Great timing, Madame Brille.* He grabbed Ava's hand and pulled her down behind a table. Everywhere people were shouting. The guards, after another moment of confusion, spread out and started forward purposefully.

Ava began to crawl under the table.

'Wait,' Howell whispered.

'For what?'

She kept going and he followed her. Fortunately, there was enough chaos and people running about that no one saw where they'd gone. They reached the far end of the table and paused there, peering out. A vast loom stood close by, churning out shimmering cloth that slithered, snake-like, down through a hole in the floor.

'There,' Howell said. His breathing echoed loudly in his ears. Holes, like mirrors, had to lead somewhere.

'You're mad. We can't go down there. We'll be killed.'

'Would you rather stay here?' He rolled out from under the table.

A guard swung round and shouted, his voice lost in the thundering of the loom. But then another man caught his arm and pointed away across the tables, sending him running in that direction.

Howell felt a shock go through him: Master Tudur. He was thinner than when Howell had seen him last, and his normally tidy clothes were torn and filthy. For a second he stood, and then he nodded to Howell and turned away.

'Thank you,' Howell whispered, knowing his old master wouldn't hear. He took The Book off Ava and shoved her hard in the back with it. She yelped and stumbled into the hole, barely managing to snatch the cloth in time. Howell grabbed hold and, as guards ran to surround him, he jumped in after her.

Machinery shrieked and grated around them until Howell felt as if his ears would burst with the noise. He buried his head in the thick folds of cloth as it juddered down, the patch of light from the hole above barely penetrating the darkness.

'Ava, are you there?'

'Where else would I be? You pushed me.'

'Sorry. I didn't think you were going to move on your own.' He reached out cautiously with a foot and touched something solid. They were in a chute of sorts, heading straight down.

The cloth jerked to a stop and the sound of machinery died away, leaving an echo that thumped in Howell's head as he dangled. He clenched his teeth. 'I'm going to climb down to you. Stay where you are.'

He began to ease his way through, edging past Ava as she clung tight to the folds of cloth. His eyes adjusted quickly to the dark – he could see the shadowy mass of fabric now, and when he looked up, the paler patch of Ava's face as she gazed down at him.

The chute widened and Howell's feet sank into something soft: cloth, piled up, fold on top of fold. He stumbled free, trying to shake some feeling back into his hands. In the faint shimmering light of magic on the cloth he could just make out walls around him and scattered bits of leaves and dead grass on the floor.

Ava dropped down beside him. 'I can't see a thing. Where are we?'

'I don't know. It looks like a cellar.'

'We're trapped, you mean.'

Howell shook his head. He wasn't going to believe that. He clenched his fingers into his palms, trying to breathe steadily, even though each breath made his chest tighten. Mr Bones wouldn't just dump cloth in here and leave it. There had to be a door into this room.

'Here, take The Book,' he said. He felt his way across to a wall and started pushing at the stones. Ava helped for a while, then she sat down on a heap of cloth with The Book on her knees and watched. 'How long until the guards come down?'

'I don't know.' The room seemed to be growing lighter. He kept pushing, digging his fingers between stones until his nails hurt.

'Howell,' Ava said.

He swallowed his irritation. 'Don't worry. There must be a door.'

'I know. You can stop looking for it.'

Howell turned round and all the suffocating panic pressed down on him again.

It *was* lighter in here, and the light was coming from the far wall where, slowly, the dark stones were melting into silver mist.

CHAPTER 35

When you're angry, when you're sad,
Put it in the mirror and you won't feel so bad.
Let your reflection take your pain
And you will be quite happy again.
If you're tired of hearing that rhyme, think how you'd feel if
you were Ephraim Skinner and had it ringing in your ears
for more than two hundred years. This is why you shouldn't
mess with magic mirrors.

The Book

A good policeman examines the evidence and does not jump to conclusions, but the evidence unfolding before Charles's eyes was hard to believe.

Mr Bones looked out of the mirror, his dark eyes glittering with irritation. The mob of people were all huddled together, torn between staying to see what would happen and running away as fast as they could.

'What do you mean, you're Lord Skinner's reflection?' Mr Footer demanded. 'How can you be a reflection?'

Mr Bones tilted his head to one side, smiling thinly. 'You'd be surprised what is possible with magic. Real magic, not the pale version you play with. Is this your mirror?'

'The conjuror is acting under my instructions,' Lord Skinner said. 'You will speak to me, not to him.' He tried to edge away from the mirror but the crowd pushed him back. 'Mr Footer, this creature is a fairy illusion, nothing more. You can't trust anything it says. Please be so kind as to banish it immediately.'

Mr Footer said nothing. Charles adjusted his grip on Mrs Footer so he could feel his notebook in his pocket. The solid, simple lines felt reassuring.

In the mirror, Mr Bones smirked.

'Go back,' Lord Skinner said. 'Stay on your side of the mirror, attend to your own business and leave me in peace. We agreed.'

'Yes, we agreed,' Mr Bones said. 'You rule on your side, I on mine, and whenever you summon me I will do anything you command. But you did not summon me this time.' He turned his attention back to Mr Footer and inclined his head slightly. 'Tell me what you want, conjuror. If it's in my power, I will do it. You have my word.'

Mr Footer licked his lips nervously and glanced around at the gathered townspeople. He had the look of a mouse standing before a cat, a large, magical cat that was deciding whether or not to pounce.

Mrs Footer trembled and whined. Her hair was standing on end, and Charles was sure his own was about to do the same. The skin across the back of his neck prickled fiercely. 'Ask him where Mrs Footer is,' he called.

Mr Footer gulped and nodded. 'Mr Bones, I command you to find my mother.' His voice squeaked nervously.

A slow, triumphant smile spread across Mr Bones's face. No, this wasn't good. Charles wasn't sure what Mr Footer had done exactly, but Mr Bones shouldn't be looking so pleased.

'At last,' Mr Bones breathed.

He put a hand on his side of the mirror, spread his fingers, and pushed.

The glass bulged beneath his palm. A small, clouded patch appeared and quickly grew bigger until half the mirror was white with mist, and, through it, Charles saw the dark, thin shape of Mr Bones.

His hand came through the mist first, emerging into Waning Crescent. A few people screamed as he wiggled his fingers. One lady fainted.

'You gave your word!' Mr Footer shouted.

Mr Bones's face appeared through the mist. 'You ordered me to find your mother. I am obeying.'

The mist around him parted. Charles watched, unable to look away as Mr Bones stepped all the way through the mirror and stood in the hallway of Waning Crescent.

'Go back!' Lord Skinner shrieked. 'I command you!'

Mrs Footer buried her head under Charles's jacket, whining softly.

A cold wind rushed above Charles's head. Every candle in every chandelier, every candleholder, fluttered wildly and went out.

In the darkened hall one voice spoke, and that voice was as dark and quiet as the grave. 'You don't command me now.'

Observe, Charles thought desperately. *A good investigator observes the evidence.* He tried to stop the trembling in his legs. In the pale scraps of moonlight that made it through the windows, Charles saw Mr Bones advancing through the hall. His clothes stretched oddly over him, not quite fitting – possibly because the body beneath wasn't quite body-shaped. He didn't wear a hat, and his dark hair, which had lain flat before now, drifted up in wisps to meet the mist that circled him.

There was no sound at all now, except for Lord Skinner moaning.

Mr Bones turned suddenly and fixed his gaze on Charles. 'What are you afraid of, boy?' he murmured.

Charles thought his heart was going to explode. He swallowed and found his voice. 'Right now? You.'

Mr Bones laughed. 'You should be.' He sprang.

'Charles!' Mrs Brunel screamed.

Charles shut his eyes tight.

He didn't die. He felt bony hands on his arms, tugging Mrs Footer out of his jacket.

'Here is your mother,' Mr Bones said.

Charles risked opening his eyes. Mr Bones was holding Mrs Footer up, and then he threw her into Mr Footer's arms.

The conjuror staggered back with a surprised 'Oof' and sat down. Shadows coiled around him and the air filled with the scent of lavender. A moment later, instead of the dog, Mr Footer was holding his mother on his lap. Her bonnet hung half off, her hair stood in disarray and her dress was full of holes, but she was alive and back in her proper shape. She scrambled up, red-faced.

'It really *was* you,' Mr Footer said.

Mrs Footer took her bonnet off and hit him with it. 'Of course it was me. Don't you know your own mother? Some conjuror you are. If it wasn't for the children helping me, I'd have ended up on the streets.'

Charles's face was suddenly full of his own mother's dress. 'Charles. Are you all right?'

'I'm fine, Mother.' He struggled free, half smothered, and tried to see past her.

Mr Bones stood still in the middle of the hall. The shadows around him thickened and started to take on shape – skeletal shapes.

Lord Skinner gave a loud cry and backed away.

'I am bones,' Mr Bones said, cracking his knuckles. 'I am fear given shape – everything you ever tried to hide. You put it all into the mirror and you pretended I wasn't part of you, but we are opposite halves, Ephraim Skinner: you the frightened child, and me everything that child could become if only he dared.'

Lord Skinner held up his hands, trying to ward off the sight of Mr Bones advancing on him. He backed away, losing one of his slippers and knocking over a hall table.

Mr Bones kept walking, one slow step after another. 'Still so afraid of death, Ephraim? But why would I kill you? If you die, I die. We are bound together – yet I have served you long enough.'

Charles watched, half horrified, half fascinated at the sight of the richest and most powerful man in Wyse cowering in his nightwear. He even felt a bit sorry for him.

Lord Skinner covered his face with his hands. 'Go back to Unwyse. Ava Harcourt is there, and the boy. The Book too. You can have them all. Rule the Unworld and leave me be.'

That is just cowardly, Charles thought, his sympathy disappearing. A ghostly skeleton brushed past him. He yelped and jumped back.

Lord Skinner tried to run, shoving people out of his way. They all stood frozen, too frightened to move.

Mr Bones caught up with Lord Skinner at the

door and took him by the collar.

'Conjuror,' he said to Mr Footer. 'You command me. Do you wish me to remain here?'

'Go away,' Mrs Footer snapped.

Mr Footer gulped. 'Yes, go. Go back to the Unworld where you belong and never trouble us again.'

'Wait,' Charles said in alarm, but Mr Footer didn't listen. Charles didn't think the conjuror could hear anything except his own terror.

'Go,' Mr Footer said, louder this time.

Mr Bones bowed, turned and walked back along the hall to the mirror, towing Lord Skinner behind him.

Mr Footer gaped. 'I didn't mean take him too. Let him go.'

Mr Bones looked back. 'You ordered me to go. He and I are one and the same.' He walked on.

Mist rose up to surround him. Lord Skinner didn't resist. He hung limp, a large bag dangling from Mr Bones's hand, slowly disappearing.

The mist shrank back to the size of the mirror, then the glass cleared and reflected the hall once again. Mr Bones and Lord Skinner were gone.

For a long moment, no one spoke.

Charles ran to the mirror. The glass was hard and cold again. It didn't respond, even when he prodded and then struck it with his palm.

Reverend Stowe opened the door and looked out.

Moonlight streamed across the hall, glancing off all the mirrors.

'What do we do now?' he asked.

Possibly because Mr Footer was peering at him, other people turned in Charles's direction too, as if they expected him to know. Even Constable Blackson looked at him. Charles rubbed his forehead. Ava and Howell were in Unwyse and now, thanks to Lord Skinner, Mr Bones knew.

'Make the mirror work again,' he said. 'I'm going through after them.'

'You're doing no such thing,' his mother said. 'Mr Footer, I forbid you to open that mirror.'

Mrs Footer smacked the conjuror on the arm. 'I forbid you too. You've done enough damage.'

It wouldn't help, anyway, Charles thought. You couldn't go through a mirror without an invitation, and he couldn't imagine Mr Bones inviting them across. But they couldn't just give up and go home, not after all this.

'Let's search the house,' Charles said. 'There might be more working mirrors around.' He wasn't convinced, but he'd promised Ava and Howell he'd investigate.

He didn't expect anyone to agree, but surprisingly they did. People nodded.

Mrs Footer clapped Charles on the shoulder. 'Excellent idea, young man. Let's get to it.'

CHAPTER 36

The future is about to change. I hate it when it does that.
I like to know what's going to happen, and now I have no
more idea than you. I wonder if this is what it's like to be
mortal – always worrying what might happen next.

The Book

Ava stood up slowly as the cellar wall turned to mist. Gradually the mist brightened, as if the sun was shining through it, until she could see the whole cellar, and the heap of enchanted cloth piled up behind them.

'This is not good,' Howell muttered.

Ava nodded, but the knot in her chest loosened. At least she could see now. Anything was better than waiting in the dark, not knowing what was around her.

But then the mist parted down the middle and Ava realized there was something worse than being trapped in the dark. Finding herself before Mr Bones, seeing his pale face, and his eyes – darker than the cellar had been, and full of malice: that was much, much worse.

And worse again was the thing being dragged behind him. For a second, Ava's eyes refused to see it properly and she thought it was a large bag. Then it twitched, and gave a little moan, and she realized who it was: Lord Skinner.

Ava put a hand to her mouth, stifling the cry that wanted to get out.

He was barefoot, wearing pyjamas and a gold dressing gown, which had got tangled around him. His eyelids fluttered weakly as he bumped along the floor and, when Mr Bones let go of him, he slumped into a pile as if everything inside him had been emptied out.

'Good,' Mr Bones said. 'You're here just in time.' He put out a hand. 'You can give me The Book now.'

Ava wrapped her arms round it. She could feel her heart beating against her ribs. This wasn't fair. She'd never asked to become The Book's guardian. She'd never asked for any of this to happen.

Where's your sense of adventure, Ava?

'Shut up,' she muttered to herself. Mr Bones hadn't won yet. 'Where's Matthew?' Her voice trembled. 'What have you done to him?'

Mr Bones shook his head. 'You really are quite annoying. Your brother and Lunette are safe. Come with me and I'll take you to them.'

Ava backed away from his outstretched hand. 'Why

do you want The Book anyway? It's not exactly useful.'

'Is that what you think?' His dark eyes glinted. He turned to Howell. 'We talked about this, boy. What is written must come to pass.'

Howell was suddenly still, barely breathing. 'The covenant,' he whispered. 'The covenant was written down.'

'That not exactly useful book,' Mr Bones said, 'is the book of the covenant between our two worlds – created here in Unwyse, from the same magic that sustains the mirrors, protected with magic so that nobody can write in it and change what was written. But the mirrors are failing, and The Book's magic has failed along with them. In fact, it has so little magic left now that it is almost ordinary paper again.'

The Book weighed heavily in Ava's arms. She clasped it closer, protectively. 'The Book said no one could write in it.'

'Did it? Or did it say certain people couldn't write in it? I have had two hundred years to study these things. The Book and its guardian are connected and it appears that this is enough to overcome what little magic The Book has left.' Mr Bones kicked Lord Skinner absent-mindedly. 'Or should I say The Book's *guardians*. Your brother was quick to reveal the truth when I threatened to hurt his lady friend.'

Ava was clutching The Book so tightly that her hands ached. 'You'd better not have hurt them.'

'I haven't. And I won't if you give me The Book.'

He held out his hand again.

'Don't,' Howell said.

'I'm sorry.' She hoped he'd see from her face that she wasn't going to let Mr Bones win. He couldn't make them write in The Book. They'd find a way to beat him, but for now, if they wanted to rescue Matthew and Lunette, they had to let him think he'd won.

Slowly she raised her arms and released her grip on The Book, dropping it into Mr Bones's waiting hands. He inclined his head as he accepted it.

'That wasn't so hard, was it?' he said. 'Come this way, if you please.'

Cool mist swallowed them all.

They stepped out into a room that made Ava gasp in surprise. It was an exact copy of the banqueting hall at Waning Crescent. Candles cast pools of yellow light across the wood-panelled walls. A fire crackled in the grate, but instead of warmth, it gave off an icy chill. A mirror hung above it in a pale frame – a frame made of bone, Ava saw with a shiver.

In the centre of the room, Matthew and Lunette sat either side of the long dining table, empty plates set before them.

Ava started forward. 'Matthew!'

He didn't respond. Ava shook his shoulder, but he

remained as cold and rigid as stone. 'You said he was safe,' she said accusingly.

'And so he is.' Mr Bones set The Book on the table. 'They were proving troublesome, so I put them to sleep. I'll wake them soon.' He dumped Lord Skinner next to the fire and took a pipe from the mantelpiece. Entirely unhurried, he filled and lit it. He turned to face the mirror, and Ava saw with a shock that he had no reflection. How was that possible? Everything had a reflection.

Lord Skinner pulled himself up against the mantelpiece. His whole body shook so violently that Ava wondered how he managed to stay on his feet.

'Mr Bones,' he said, 'you will remember your place. I created you and you promised to serve me. I command you to release us all.'

Ava's hands slid off Matthew's shoulders. 'You created him? What do you mean?'

'*When you're angry, when you're sad, put it in the mirror*,' Mr Bones said mockingly. 'It worked too well, didn't it, Ephraim?'

Lord Skinner moaned. 'I was ten years old when my parents died. My father left me his magic mirror. Nobody told me not to mess with it – nobody warned me what I might see. They all said I had to be brave, to be a good boy. So I remembered the rhyme. I spent whole nights in front of the mirror, pretending my reflection was the angry boy, the grieving boy, the boy who was afraid that he, too, would fall sick and die. And then, one night, the boy in the mirror looked back at me and spoke.'

Ava felt the room sway. Reflections didn't just come to life.

Howell pulled a chair out and sat down, looking dazed. He didn't seem to know what he was doing.

Mr Bones gave a terrible smile. 'Reflections are real things. An ordinary mirror shows what you look like on the outside. I am the opposite of that: I show what's on the inside. Made out of magic and all the parts of Ephraim Skinner that little Ephraim didn't want – is it any wonder he fears me?'

Lord Skinner's own fear, given shape. Ava shivered. Of course Mr Bones had no reflection of his own – he *was* a reflection.

'That must be why he vanished so suddenly from the factory floor,' Howell said softly. 'Lord Skinner looked into a magic mirror in Wyse, and Mr Bones had to appear.'

And that explained Lord Skinner using Mr Footer as a spy, Ava thought. *If he looked in a mirror himself, all he'd see would be Mr Bones.*

She looked at Lord Skinner and her stomach rolled with an odd mix of pity and horror. He'd grown up with only himself for company, he'd said. He'd meant it quite literally, and now he was at war with his own reflection.

Lord Skinner pulled his dressing gown straight. 'I'm not afraid of you, Mr Bones,' he said, fumbling with the belt. 'I command you to release us.'

Mr Bones laughed. 'You command nothing on this side of the mirror, Ephraim Skinner. Unwyse belongs to me. I'd kill you if I could, but we are tied together. I've kept you alive all these years, because death is what you fear most. You will do anything to avoid it.'

He snapped his fingers.

All around the room the candles went out. The only light now came from the fire and a silver glow at the windows. Lunette remained frozen, but Matthew jumped and stared around.

'Ava? What's going on?'

Ava threw her arms round his shoulders. 'We're fine. Don't worry.'

'No, you really should worry,' Mr Bones said. He tossed his pipe into the fireplace. Shadows stirred all around them and a sound rose, first like the rustling of dead leaves and then growing harder, less like leaves now and more like . . .

Bones.

Mist poured in through the windows and took shape. Skeletons: four of them. Their bone arms dangled at their sides, their fingers twitching restlessly. Their empty mouths hung in permanent grins; their empty eye sockets seemed to have no end: deep, dark holes, rimmed in cold white.

The Book fell open on the table. Words scrawled into being, so faint that Ava could barely read them.

The Book of Unwyse Magic containing the Covenant between the Human World and the Unworld.

These are the terms of the covenant between the Human World and the Unworld.

The Fair Folk will withdraw from the world and take all magic with them to form their own realm. Yet the Human World must not be left wholly without magic. Magic mirrors will be created, two by two, each pair forming a doorway between the Human World and the new Unworld. Any person may cross through, if invited from the other side. Furthermore, the Unworld will supply all magical goods and services requested through the mirrors.

While the mirrors stand, so shall this covenant. If it ends, the Unworld will end with it. What is written must come to pass.

If words on a page could look sad, these did.

A pair of bone pens appeared on the table, one either side of The Book.

'Guardians of The Book,' Mr Bones said, 'it is time to rewrite the covenant and change our worlds forever. You will take up these pens and write what I say.

These are the terms of the covenant, freely written. The mirrors will reawaken. The Human World will serve the Unworld forever.' He smiled grimly. 'And this bag of skin will serve me,' he added.

The skeletons moved closer. 'Write or you will all die,' Mr Bones said. He pointed at Matthew. 'Starting with him.'

Matthew stood up. 'Try it.'

'Matthew, don't!' Ava cried. She clasped her hands behind her back, twisting her fingers together until they hurt, afraid she'd reach for the pen.

Mr Bones put a hand on her shoulder. His grip froze her. 'You might as well do what I say. You can't make things worse than you already have. If it wasn't for you, your brother would be safe and happy, living his own life. If it wasn't for you, Howell would have his own magic, but you stole it. How many other lives have you ruined?'

Ava tried to look away from him, but she couldn't. She was falling into a deep, black hole with nothing to cling on to. It was true. It was no wonder people regarded her with suspicion and whispered behind her back. They knew there was something wrong with her.

'And you,' Mr Bones continued, turning to Howell. 'Do you want to stay here forever? Year after year in Waxing Gibbous, doing the most tedious jobs until boredom turns your thoughts to dust?'

Howell clenched his hand until his fingers turned as white as the bone pen. A drop of crimson ink formed at the tip and dropped on to the table.

'I am bones,' Mr Bones murmured, standing between them both. 'I am the fear you try to hide. You can cover me over for a time, but you can never get rid of me. I am your greatest terrors given shape, and I cannot be stopped. Nobody can help you. Write or stay here forever forgotten. Write, or your brother will die.'

Ava felt a low sob rise in her chest. If she wrote what Mr Bones wanted, she'd be ruining the lives of everyone in the world. But if she didn't write he'd kill Matthew. She reached for the pen.

Then a voice spoke out of the wall. 'Excuse me, Mr Bones, but you're wrong.'

CHAPTER 37

You know I told you once you ought to stop reading and run for help? Now might be a good time to do it. I think the worlds are about to change.

The Book

Ava turned her head and froze, staring in amazement. Charles! Charles was looking out at her through the mirror over the fire. She thought it was another trick until he grinned and waved, and his expression was so Charles-like that she knew it really was him. The shadows that had invaded her mind fled away, allowing her to think clearly again. She pushed Mr Bones's hand off her shoulder.

'Charles, what are you doing?' she asked.

Charles flipped his hair out of his eyes. 'We searched Waning Crescent and we found a mirror hidden upstairs in a room full of rubbish. And I thought: we have three conjurors here so we might as well see if we can get it to work. He spread his arms. 'And – ta-dah!'

Mr Bones made a noise like knuckles cracking.

Charles had worked a mirror? Not just any mirror, but Lord Skinner's secret mirror. Ava hadn't even dared try it for fear of where it might lead.

'I didn't do it on my own,' Charles said. 'Mrs Footer took charge – she's back to herself again. And quite a lot of the town are here too.'

Various hands waved behind him in the glass. Ava waved back, a smile growing on her lips. Everyone there, wanting to help.

She felt The Book move and she looked down at it. A single word was beginning to form, letter by letter.

C o n n e c

The page went blank.

Connection. Everything was connected. She was connected to Matthew by blood, connected to Howell by magic, and to Charles by friendship. Just as Lord Skinner and Mr Bones were connected by that mirror.

Mr Bones's eyes burned. 'Write,' he said. 'I will give you everything that belonged to Lord Skinner. Wealth and power. You can put right all the damage you have done. You won't need to be afraid again.'

Is that what he'd promised Lord Skinner once? Ava's gaze slid to the trembling old man. For a moment, she saw him as a boy, lonely and afraid. He'd thought he was getting rid of his fears, but they'd come alive and taken over.

It's better to be shaped by our kindness than our

fears. Who'd said that? Reverend Stowe? Ava choked out a laugh. She could barely breathe, but she had to laugh because fear only existed if it had something to feed off – just like a skeleton couldn't exist without its body, and a reflection couldn't exist without a mirror.

'Charles,' Ava said. 'Break the mirror.'

His eyes grew round in the glass. 'What? But you'll be trapped.'

'No we won't. Trust me.'

'Stop them,' Mr Bones snapped. The skeletons sprang forward.

Charles's face disappeared from the mirror. The glass misted over, then turned grey. Mr Bones staggered, but stayed on his feet. Charles might have broken his mirror, but the connection between the two wouldn't break until both mirrors were shattered.

Ava turned, looking for something to throw, but a skeleton caught her round the waist.

'Help!' she shouted, struggling.

Lunette stirred and jumped up. Matthew tried to drag the skeleton away, but it swung round and clubbed him back with one arm. He crashed into the table, his face twisted in pain.

Mr Bones forced a pen into Ava's hand. 'Write, or your brother dies.'

Ava closed her eyes so she wouldn't have to see what happened next. Matthew shouted. A chair broke. A cold hand clutched at her neck and squeezed.

She struggled to breathe.

Something cracked.

Ava thought it was her neck breaking. But the hand round her throat loosened. She opened her eyes and found herself staring straight into the face of a skeleton, so close the skull was almost touching her. And then, as she struggled to breathe air into her lungs to scream, the bone face splintered. White dust poured from the eye sockets, its mouth gaped and then its jaw fell off altogether. The hands released her, bits of finger bone clinging to her a moment longer before they, too, crumbled.

Ava picked herself up, shaking.

Lord Skinner stood by the fireplace, the remains of a chair in his hands. The mirror behind him was a mass of cracks. A piece of glass teetered and fell, smashing into bits on the floor with a barely audible whisper.

Lord Skinner dropped the chair. His face was the colour of dead leaves. 'There,' he said.

Mr Bones swayed. 'Why?'

Lord Skinner shook his head. Some of his hair fell out with the movement.

'I'm tired,' he mumbled. 'So tired of being afraid all the time. Miss Harcourt, I'm sorry.'

He met Ava's gaze and just for a second or two she saw a young boy, his face screwed up and wet with angry tears. Then, gently, Lord Skinner crumpled down on to the floor, shrinking into himself, his hair now pure white, and his skin turning blotched and mottled with age. Hair and skin fell away, leaving a heap of grey bones, and then the bones disappeared too until there was nothing left but his dressing gown lying in a limp, gold bundle on the carpet.

Mr Bones cried out. No longer terrifying, just the reflection of a frightened boy brought to life. And, like all reflections, he couldn't exist on its own. He remained a moment longer, then, as another piece of glass slid from the mirror, he faded, first to a shadowy skeleton, and then to nothing at all.

Matthew moved first. 'Ava.' He ran to her and hugged her tight enough to squash the remaining air out of her.

Ava scrubbed tears from her face. 'I'm fine. Can we please go home now?'

'We haven't finished,' Howell said. He held up a pen. 'We are still The Book's guardians.'

He ran a hand over The Book. The yellow pages were turning brown at the corners. The Book was dying, Ava thought. They could fix that. They could bring the mirrors back to life and The Book, made from the same magic, would revive too.

What was written must come to pass, she thought. This was why they were really here: to rewrite the covenant.

Ava picked up a pen and set it down again. 'No. What if we get it wrong? Look at everything else I've ruined. Mr Bones was right about that.'

'You didn't ruin anything,' Howell said. He scratched the top of one ear, his eyes shining. 'You didn't steal my magic, we shared it – and now we can do something no one else can do. We can bring mirrors back to life. And we're the guardians of The Book, which means we're guardians of the covenant. I wouldn't have any of that without you.'

Ava's eyes swam with tears all over again. She dashed them away.

'And if you think I'd be better off without you, you don't know very much,' Matthew said. 'Without you, I'd be all on my own.' He reached for Lunette's hand.

They were all looking at her as if they really meant what they were saying. Ava found herself smiling back at them.

'What should we write?' she asked.

Howell bent his head close and whispered to her.

After a moment, Ava nodded and picked up the pen. She wished everyone in Wyse could see this happening, but they'd find out soon enough.

'Ready?' Howell asked.

'Ready.'

They wrote.

These are the terms of the covenant between the Human World and the Unworld.

The first covenant is fulfilled. There is no more obligation. Humans and Fair Folk alike may cross through the mirrors when invited.

What is written must come to pass.

The writing darkened and writhed on the pages of The Book. For a moment, the words of the old covenant appeared again, but they faded away.

The Book shrugged its pages.

Hello, guardians. Everything feels different. Did we win?

CHAPTER 38

The town of Wyse, set precisely on the border of England and Wales, is remarkable. It is the only human town twinned with the Unworld, where Fair Folk visit for holidays, and fairy enchantments are traded for hat pins. Or it will be in the second half of the nineteenth century. As for other time periods, don't ask me: I'm only a book.

The Book

Charles Brunel spent the next day in Waning Crescent. Half the townspeople did. Children ran through the halls, laughing; older people argued over who would get the best furniture, while the town conjurors examined the mirrors and tried to make them work. They succeeded with two. Mr Footer's mirror showed the face of the blue-haired fairy girl who informed them, rather snappishly, that things were changing and they'd need to wait. Another mirror hanging in the hall appeared to open into an empty room, with sheets lying all over the floor, where a frightened green-haired boy told them he didn't know what was going on, but none of it was his fault.

Mrs Footer, who seemed remarkably less snappish than before, bustled from room to room, stopping people stealing things and occasionally scolding the children if they made too much noise. The whole thing was quite festive, rather like a holiday, Charles thought. The mist was clearing too, and Reverend Stowe reported that holidaymakers were drifting back into town and complaining that no conjurors were available to perform for them.

Charles wished Ava and Howell were here to see all this.

'I'm sure they're fine,' his mother said.

'I know they are.' Ava could take care of herself, Charles thought. Besides, the mist was finally clearing from the streets and there'd been no further trouble from magical intruders, so he guessed Mr Bones must have been defeated.

He had to wait until the next evening before he found out. He was back home writing up his case notes when he heard a knock at the door and, a moment later, his sisters' twin shrieks of surprise.

Ava and Howell stood on the doorstep, both of them jigging with excitement. Matthew and Lunette waited behind them, hand in hand, and with them was a green-haired man Charles had never seen before.

'Hello, Charles,' Ava said. 'I'm sorry we're late, but you wouldn't believe the trouble we had getting home. First we had to find our way out from beneath Waxing Gibbous, and then it took ages to persuade people in the factory that Mr Bones was dead and they could go. And then we had to break mirror seventy-seven because that's the one that was letting the mist through into Wyse. Howell did tell Will to break it, but he wouldn't. He thought it'd be bad luck or something. Anyway, it's all sorted now.' She paused for breath.

'This is Master Tudur,' Howell said, pushing the green-haired man forward. 'He's taken over the Mirror Station in Unwyse and we need to talk about what's going to happen next.'

They all looked at Charles expectantly. Ava and Howell had gabbled so much that Charles didn't have the first idea what they'd just said.

'You'd better come in,' he said. 'What *is* going to happen next?'

Ava glanced at Howell. 'I've got some ideas, but I think we should all decide together.'

It was the first time Ava had ever attended a town meeting, and she wasn't expecting to enjoy it, but she did. Everyone seemed much friendlier. Even Mrs Footer told her she was a useful girl and said Ava might wish to call her Aunt Lily in private. Ava smiled to herself. Reverend Stowe had told them to give it a week or two and they'd be feeling at home here, though Ava doubted he'd meant it quite like this.

At first, the shopkeepers and hotel owners weren't happy that their source of income was gone. Who would visit Wyse now that the town no longer had a steady supply of fairy enchantments? But then Matthew stood up and presented their idea.

'Ava and Howell can bring magic mirrors back to life,' he said. 'What if they did it – but only in Wyse and Unwyse. We will be the official – the only – crossing point between this world and the Unworld. We can use Waning Crescent as our own Mirror Station and we'll employ people to look after the mirrors. We can have proper passports and travel documents, and we can trade goods through the mirrors. We can still get enchantments – better enchantments, even – and the Unworld can have . . . chocolate, and tea, and things like that.'

'Hat pins,' Lunette said. 'Hat pins are always useful.'

And then everyone was talking. Ava didn't mind that they all seemed to have forgotten her: she'd have plenty to do soon, by the sound of it. She slid her hand under the pew and took out The Book, opening it between her and Howell.

'What do you think, Book?' she asked.

The pages moved in a little wave.

What do I think? I think you two can bring the

mirrors back to life. The future is up to you now: there are far too many possibilities for me to untangle them all. Whatever happens, though, I predict it will be fun.

ACKNOWLEDGEMENTS

After writing two swashbuckling adventures, a Victorian mystery was quite a challenge and the past year has been a bit like learning to write all over again. This story would never have been completed without the guidance of my wonderful editors, Julia and Lucy. Thank you, both of you! A big thank you, also, to everyone at Henry Holt and Macmillan Children's Books who have supported me from the beginning. I couldn't ask for a better team.

Thank you, Becka Moor for the brilliant UK artwork.

The idea for this book came out of a conversation I had with my agent, Gemma Cooper. Gemma, you know how much I appreciate you, but thank you once again for sparking my imagination.

Thank you, everyone who read my rough drafts and helped me to point the story in the right direction. Special thanks are due to Stephanie Burgis and Robin Stevens who read this book early on and said such lovely things about it. And thank you to Team Cooper and the many writing friends and colleagues who have given me such good advice.

Thank you, as always, to my husband, Phillip, and my friends who keep me going with coffee and cake and put up with me rambling about made-up worlds. I'm not going to list you all again, but you know who you are.

A large part of this book was written in the Coffi House in Cardiff and the staff there deserve a special mention for their friendly service and excellent, giant mugs of coffee.

Thank you to all the readers who have been in touch with me – I love hearing from you. And to the booksellers, librarians, schools, book bloggers, all the wonderful people who support children's books. You are changing the lives of so many children. Thank you!

Turn the page for an extract of . . .

STORM HOUND

The next book from

CLAIRE FAYERS

falling from the skies in 2019

He was Storm of Odin, last-born hound of the Wild Hunt that runs across the plains of the sky on stormy nights. He was barely four months old, but almost as tall as the crimson-tailed horses that raced before him. His coat was black as the deepest midnight, his eyes shone golden-bright, alive with excitement.

He was Storm of Odin and this was his first hunt. He opened his mouth and howled, his voice joining the cries of the pack around him. The scream of hunting horns echoed between the wide horizons and moonlight glanced off the hunters' helmets and the tips of their spears. Sky and earth trembled.

He was Storm of Odin, and . . .

. . . and he was having a little trouble keeping up.

He ran as fast as ever – faster in fact, because he was straining now, his muscles beginning to ache, and the wild joy of the Hunt was being overtaken by an uneasy feeling. He dropped his head and his howls became a series of pants and grunts as he struggled to keep his legs moving. The crimson horse-tails were no longer in his face but flickered in the darkness ahead like distant glimmers of flame.

The stormhound slowed, and his paws began to sink through the cloud beneath him. He howled again, his voice less like thunder now, more like a cry of 'Hey, wait for me!'

No one heard. No one waited.

The Wild Hunt rushed on.

Behind them all, Storm of Odin uttered a final yelp and fell from the sky.

Morning came and brought a headache with it. The sunlight made everything bright and sharp-edged – much bigger than he'd expected it. The sky, no longer thunder-filled, was a clear, light grey, speckled with white wisps that didn't deserve the name of clouds. Mountains rose in indistinct humps all around while, closer by, trees towered over him, their branches hung with brown leaves. More leaves crackled beneath his paws as he took his first step.

But where was he?

The only creatures in sight were a huddle of sheep staring at him from a field on the other side of a grey stripe on the ground. A 'road' – he'd heard the huntsmen speak of them. Humans had built them because they didn't have horses to carry them. Instead, they crawled along these grey paths in armoured shells like snails.

The stormhound stepped onto the road to look about him. The surface was rough, surprisingly hard, and smelled of warm stones and tar. A large sign stood almost opposite him.

Y Fenni 5

Abergavenny 5

The shapes meant nothing to him. And why weren't

4

the sheep fleeing from him in terror? Or falling at his feet in awe? Were they so stupid that they didn't know who he was?

Hey! Sheep! the stormhound shouted.

The sheep gazed blankly at him, chewing grass. Eventually, one of them wandered closer. *You talking to us?*

Who else I would I be talking to? A growl rose in Storm of Odin's throat as he prowled forward a step. *I am Storm of Odin of the Wild Hunt. Did you not hear us pass by last night?*

The sheep looked at one another and back at him. *If you're a stormhound,* said the one who'd spoken before, *I'm Aries. The Ram – get it?*

And I'm Ramesses of Egypt, another one baaed. The whole flock fell about laughing.

Storm of Odin growled again in annoyance. *You're not even rams. You're just stupid sheep.*

The sheep only laughed harder.

Caaaaaaar! one of them shouted.

The stormhound shook his head. *Don't you mean baaaaa?*

The ground trembled. Storm of Odin leaped backwards just in time. A rush of air, a noise like thunder and something metal roared by on the road. It was vast – the size of several chariots put together, and almost as loud as the Wild Hunt.

A moment later it was gone.

The stormhound rolled over and came up coughing. The air tasted of smoke and oil.

Car, the sheep said smugly. The rest of the flock chewed grass frantically, looking as if they were trying not to laugh.

Another of the metal things rushed into sight and shot by, faster and noisier than anything the stormhound had seen in his short life.

What do you get if you cross a stormhound and a sheep? one of the sheep asked. *A very baaaaaaad dog. Go back to the sky, storm puppy. It's not safe here.*

Storm puppy? Storm of Odin growled at the insult. He put a paw on the road, intending to cross over and teach the sheep a lesson, but he felt another rumble begin to build and he stepped back. Odin would smite the sheep for their insolence when the Hunt returned. He turned his back on the sheep with as much dignity as he could muster and began to walk.

Then, unexpectedly, one of the metal shells swerved to the side of the road and stopped.

Storm of Odin drew back, a low growl rumbling in his throat as a door opened in the side and a man stepped out.

The stormhound fell silent in surprise.

The man was huge. So tall, Storm of Odin could barely see his face. Rain fell on his bare head and soaked into his clothes – long trousers and a shirt of such thin cloth it wouldn't stop the stab of a thorn, never mind spears and arrows.

The stormhound scuttled backwards on his bottom. This was far worse than he'd thought. He hadn't fallen into the world of men, after all, but a land of giants!

The giant squatted and stretched out a hand, palm down. 'It's all right.'

No, it wasn't all right. It was very not all right. The world was not supposed to be this big.

Unless . . .

Oh no.

The thought had been knocking quietly for his attention for some time, but Storm of Odin hadn't wanted to let it in. Now, it overwhelmed him. He looked down at the earth, at his two front paws, glossy black and quite small among the grass. He felt one of his ears flop sideways and though he growled with effort, he couldn't make it stand up again.

This man was not a giant: Storm of Odin was small. This world had shrunk him. The stormhound let out a whimper of despair.

The man lifted him out of the grass with hands that smelled of mint and soap. Storm of Odin bared his teeth.

'You're a fierce little thing, aren't you?' the man said, and ruffled the stormhound's black ears.

This was worse humiliation than anything so far. When the great Lord Odin got to hear about this he would smite this man and his tin shell

7

from the face of the earth.

The man seemed completely unaware that he was perilously close to invoking the wrath of the storm god. 'What kind of person would abandon a puppy?' he asked.

The Wild Hunt, that's who. But it wasn't their fault I got left behind and they'll be back soon, so if you will kindly release me and be on your way I will consider asking Odin not to smite your home and family with thundery vengeance.

The man clearly didn't understand a word. Instead of putting Storm of Odin down on the ground, he carried him to the metal shell and placed him gently on the back seat. Then he produced a blanket and proceeded to dry the stormhound's wet coat.

A fluffy blanket. Pink, printed all over with kittens and smelling of cat.

This was too much. Storm of Odin shook himself free and stood up, ready to enact his own thundery vengeance here and now, but the man had already let him go and was climbing into the front seat of the metal shell.

'Hold tight, little guy,' he said.

Little guy? Eat lightning, human!

The metal shell rumbled and lurched. The stormhound's stomach lurched with it. On second thoughts, he'd just lie here and chew the man's blanket for a while. That'd teach him.